CAMDEN

BLOOD VENGEANCE

CAMDEN

The last twelve hours of my human life began with a screaming match between myself and my first love.

Or maybe not.

Perhaps the end of my life began when Ryan Obeshaw met me in the North Florida University parking lot. Once he saw me, he couldn't help but talk about the string of murders that had gripped the throat of Jacksonville, Florida that spring.

I mention it, because the topic proves the freak occurrence I believed would soon dissolve from public attention hadn't done so, at all.

While I waited to pick up Markeya, I thought quietly I should've worn a hat, and a hoodie I could zip to the top of my neck. But I had left home before I could think of it.

Professors gawked at me as they passed. I was clean shaven, buzzcut, and back from Marine boot camp. Even in the light of all that, I could've appeared to be the perfect university student, if not for the visible tattoos. If it weren't for that, I don't think they would've noticed me. The smallest divergence from normalcy tied Avondale residents into sailor knots. Made them wonder whether you were some up-to-no-good interloper disguised as a civil resident. But I couldn't blame them. I was on edge too.

Any odd appearing person could be the slasher as far as I knew. As far as we all knew.

The recent news about the high-profile murders had everyone skittish. But the body count of the butcher hadn't worked alone to scare everyone shitless. The methods they used, the state they left the bodies in, did most of the work. Couple that with the victims' lack of physical similarities. The only thing any of them had in common was a measure of power, whether that power was as high as a city mayor or as modest as a construction superintendent. The only link police found was their leadership roles.

A couple of students in colorful hoodies shuffled past me. Phone speakers pumped out the voice of University President Rich Dewey. I heard every word, though I tried very hard not to listen.

"- because of recent events the Duval County school district has canceled all classes and extracurricular activities including ALHS volunteer program until further notice. This morning the governor of Florida Carson Mack and his wife were found murdered inside their private residence in Tallahassee. The state of Florida believes the nation is under attack, a state of emergency has been declared and a 6pm curfew for all citizens has been implemented---."

All classes were canceled in the middle of the day. Such a thing I'd never heard before. Markeya texted me around noon to pick her up early.

I realized the city was officially on lock down. Students clad in the maroon and black university gear hustled to their rides. Everyone had a look of hopelessness in their eyes.

I saw Ryan Obeshaw trekking with his head down, eyes glued to his phone from the main campus entrance. I yelled out to him. Ryan raised his head, jet-black dreaded hair braided down his scalp, maroon jacket flapping in the wind.

He smiled when he spotted me and once he was close enough, he embraced me. Ryan was a hugger, and a talker and the smartest twenty-year-old Earth. A Biomedical science major. He could've gone to any school in the country but wanted to stay close to his dad who'd recently started drinking again.

I'd just hung out with Ryan the day before at my parent's home in Avondale. We played five hours of Assassin's Creed in a single afternoon, and I felt nearly normal again, like bootcamp never happened. Like crawling through mud and breaking my mind and body into microscopic pieces and forcefully putting myself back together never happened. It was the first time I felt like an average pizza-gobbling, soda-guzzling nineteen-year-old in months.

"Damn you look like a Tiktok 'After' picture." Ryan smirked at my new haircut. "Tell me, just this once, was it like that movie Jarhead?"

I scowled at him. "Yes, Ry. It was just like the movie."

He rolled his eyes at my sarcasm and waved his phone in front of my face. "Now this is some fucked up shit, isn't it?" I saw a CNN news journal open on his screen. I swiped the hand away and pushed my hand across the cool plain of my head. Ryan played off his fears as well as I did. We were alike in many ways which may have facilitated the start of our friendship in the third grade. He was a strong minded individual and would've made a great marine himself, but I could tell if no one else could when he was bothered.

"For how long did you say you were back?" In that startling way he always demanded information. He always sounded like a surveyor gathering research when he asked questions. Like he was interviewing subjects.

"One more week, then schooling."

Ryan shook his head and gave a heavy sigh. I stood up straight. "What is it, now?"

"You heard about what happened in Georgia, right?"

I swallowed. "Yeah, I heard."

"What happened this morning to the Governor?"

I wanted to end the conversation now. The governor of Florida was dead. How could a thing like that take place in today's society? I scanned the crowd for Markeya. "I know what's happening."

He regarded me carefully for a moment. "You have to get Markeya out of here."

"Don't you think I know that?"

We were supposed to leave Jacksonville in three months and move near the Florida Culinary Institute in West Palm Beach. Should've been far enough away from…whatever this was. The killer had insulated themselves only to counties in North Florida. Panama City, Marianna, Pensacola.

In my daydreams, I pictured our modest apartment equipped with extravagant kitchen appliances and a row of potted herbs in the windowsill. I yearned to do what I felt destined to do and return alive to a flour-dusted Markeya. I had hoped it was what she would desire too. And I had hoped we'd be moving under better circumstances rather than because the Earth was melting and a psycho was on the loose.

"You think the governor had all of his blood jarred up too?" Ryan prodded. "At least we can skip class, huh? My parents are probably going to rush us back to Manchester for good. How the fuck do you get blood in a jar anyway?"

I cleared my throat. I didn't want to think about it. I didn't want to think about drained bodies and blood glinting in glass like molasses or fruit preserves. These murders disturbed me like nothing had in a long time.

"I don't know how to get blood into a jar after killing a guy and his wife," I told Ryan. "But however you do it, it takes determination."

"No doubt," Ryan said. "If the country isn't under siege, I don't know what's happening. But what's with the blood? Why blood? Most terrorists will just blow up government buildings to high hell. Most of the time somebody takes credit for it. Honestly, maybe it is just a serial killer with high government clearance. Could you imagine? A secret service agent losing his mind and going camp crystal lake on American society. That's a high stress job, I wouldn't be surprised."

"A serial killer who can walk through walls, then," I replied, glaring skeptically at my friend. "Every person they killed had security, and no one saw anything or they aren't alive to tell."

"What did your dad say?"

I shrugged, "He's not home yet." Sergio had been in Washington for the past two months. I wondered then if he'd been privy to happenings in Florida at all.

The conversation had begun to tie knots in my stomach, and I leaned against the car, wanting to wake up. My car was a black Volkswagen. I thought it was cool, practical. Now I wished it was a tank.

I saw Markeya approaching, a vision of light. Gold poured into a fitted white button-up and black skirt. A jacket slung over one arm, exotic bronze curls poured over her shoulders like dazzling liquid in the sunlight.

She walked right up and hugged Ryan as I hit the button on the key fob and unlocked the doors. Ryan made a nervous sniffing sound then laughed.

Markeya and I both gazed quizzically

"What?" I said.

"I'll probably never see you guys again after this. I love you."

My brows drew down, and I chuckled. "Get a grip, Ry. We're not facing the end of days. I'll see you when your parents mail you back to America."

Ryan grinned, his eyes glinting with a depth of laughter. "I'm counting on it."

"Be safe, Ry." Markeya waved him goodbye then stepped closer to me, her smile lighting up my whole world.

I pulled her into my arms and asked: "And how was your day, chef?"

Squeezing the tattoo on my arm, she snickered girlishly against my lips, I tasted a bit of warm lip gloss. "Better now."

For a moment, I felt complete contentment—at least she was smiling again. She didn't sound too happy in her text. She'd sounded frenetic and nerve-wracked. **They said the governor's DEAD. classes are canceled, what does this mean?? Please come and get me. I can't be alone right now.**

I hoisted her off the ground and swirled her around, her legs encircling me tight. I placed her on the warm car hood, softly caressed her stocking-clad thighs. I loved when she wore stockings, my touch glided easier up her legs, and they posed a bit of a challenge. I planted light kisses on her lips. This felt normal at least. Kissing and touching Markeya still made my head fill with curse words and my dick stand at attention. "You look stressed." I said.

Suddenly, the glee in her eyes extinguished, like someone had blown out her inner flame. The heat and smolder turned to ice.

"You okay?" I raised her chin.

She blinked away, squeezed the sides of my waist. "I need to talk to you about something," she said, her voice barely audible over the chaos swirling around us.

"Okay." I couldn't help but chuckle nervously despite the tension. "It's not about the governor, is it?" I asked cautiously, not sure if I wanted to hear the answer.

Her face twisted. "No. Can we just get in the car? All of this commotion about the attacks is making everything worse."

"What's 'everything'?" I said lightly, still feeling uneasy inside.

"Cam, please."

I helped her gingerly down from the hood of the car, ushered her to the passenger seat, and buckled her in.

The parking lot was nearly empty by the time I pressed the start engine button.

Markeya threw her jacket and backpack into the backseat. "I'm sleeping at Kayla's on the southside tonight, so let's just get straight on the highway."

"What was that smell?" I asked.

"What are you talking about?" Her deep brown eyes flitted to me.

I couldn't describe what I was talking about. I couldn't describe the sweet tang of bitter fruit that wafted into my nose just as Markeya reached back to toss her items into the back seat. The sudden rush of fragrance caused a click in my throat, and to my horror, I felt an overpowering urge to...

"Nothing," I said. "It's gone."

Ten minutes later, I had pulled up to Markeya's friend Nicky Henry's house. I watched her walk through the front door, her head down, eyes red-rimmed from crying before I finally drove away. Our conversation had gone nowhere but south.

When I arrived at my parents' estate, I was met with more sobering news. When the leaders started dying, my father was called back to D.C. to head the investigations for the Secret Service. It was necessary as the killings began to mount up the food chain of command towards the nation's chief. But these murders or band of murderers couldn't in a lifetime attack the President of the United States. Logically speaking, the idea was preposterous, but many preposterous things had been happening.

Giovanna cooked a fricassee, but our chef didn't want to come in anymore. In fact, half the hired staff for the Paratus estate had abandoned us. Sergio had ordered bars on our windows and extra security cameras around the perimeter, but that failed to convince anyone of their safety. I ate dinner with mom in the normally boisterous but now quiet and empty home. The echo of our forks on the plates seemed to tunnel the 5,000 square feet. That's when my exasperated mother let out a huff, and dinner ended with swiftly gathering dishes and silverware.

I retired to the loft and retrieved the pregnancy test Markeya had given me from my waist band

Sometimes I struggle to remember the last thing Markeya said to me. Not when I found her half drained in the Henrys' living room after hours of searching the crumbling upscale neighborhood for the girl my soul adored.

I mean, what was the last thing she said before she got out of my car once we pulled to a stop at Kayla Henry's mailbox. After handing me that pregnancy test? After the tears on her brown cheeks dried in thin black lines of melted mascara. I remembered her voice from the passenger seat as I stared at the two little red lines. If I could rewind to that moment, I would, again and again until I got the words right.

The summer of our sophomore year, when I convinced the teacher's pet of third period culinary class to go out with me, I had pictured something like this. Before then, I'd never known Markeya existed at school, and had never even laid eyes on her before. And never would have if I hadn't screwed up my course selection that summer. Woodworking was filled by the time I got around to choosing electives. Culinary class was the only other option that interested me. I saw it as a way to grift my GPA and pilfer free snacks on an irregular basis.

"You can't just eat all the food and not prep *something*." Markeya had groused at me after the third time Mr. Sparks partnered us up and assigned us to one of the mini test kitchens.

"I prepped." I retorted, peering at her from behind while leaning on one of the counters and eating icing out of the measuring cup.

"You have to pitch in, Paratus, shred the carrots with more care at least.."

"Sorry, mom. I'm tired from wrestling practice. I'm sore." I licked the spoon. It was a lie. I didn't know what sore muscles felt like.

Markeya glared at me. Crossing the space on my side of the kitchen to place a bowl of batter under an electric mixer. "You're lazy is what you are. I'm going to make this carrot cake you're going to eat it all. A lazy sweet tooth."

"Correct." I smiled at her. That day she had her hair pulled back in a plastic clip, little baby hairs swirled around her face. I ached to say something really stupid. At the time, annoying girls I liked was my favorite way to flirt. Their annoyance was usually pretense, but fun anyway. Markeya refused to play along. She was too mature and focused, too adult and altogether out of my league. She wore heeled boots to school, dressed like a board member of a startup.

She would only talk to me about important things in class. My preparations for up-coming wrestling meets, what internships she planned to pursue after graduation, and the difference between blanching and boiling. She made me wish I took life just as seriously, however I sensed she enjoyed our dissimilarity.

To be the critical one around someone her age whom it didn't affect or intimidate gave her a boost, or maybe relief. She told me once she looked up to my confidence, whether that confidence was mostly an affectation or not. And in turn I could be flippant and make her day adventitiously fun, a win in my book. But what had been on the tip of my tongue for weeks before the carrot cake assignment could've unraveled us in a split second. I dream about you.

I bit back on my lip, as I watched her focused profile on the rapidly whirling mixer.

"I'm not lazy," I muttered. "Your little ass is just bossy as hell."

I caught the tiny smile lifting up one corner of her lips. I tucked it away on a shelf in my mind.

I placed the measuring cup next to me on the small microwave oven and walked closer to her. She didn't look up, she didn't react at all. But I sensed a slow-moving rigidity crackling through her form.

She gave me a secret little side glance. "What do you want?" her lips barely moved.

I took the hand she had been using to hold the mixer still. The machine stopped abruptly. And then she went very, unmistakably still. Her gaze raised and melted into mine.

"I want you to go out with me?" That's what we used in Avondale Preparatory to mean any number of things. But I meant only one thing. We'd been sort of friends, but I never wanted to be friends. Not even that first day of class when I was assigned the seat next to her and we were immediately at odds on how to put out an electrical fire.

Later Markeya kept on this running joke that she only said yes because of my voice. "I always thought you were tall and yes, hot, but it's mostly the voice. I felt like you were a vampire and you were glamoring me."

"Glamouring?" I laughed the first time.

"Yes, Cam. You glamor people with your voice. I love your voice... and your hands."

Even she had her silly moments and her guilty pleasures. She was a romance at heart. A huge Anne Rice fan. A Trueblood binge watcher. Kept all the complete series of the Vampire Chronicles underneath her bed.

The first year was remarkably easy. We had no expectations. I was simply riding my lucky wave of having someone so talented, beautiful, and caring in life. But inevitably our relationship grew more serious as graduation, college applications approached. I remember it was the weekend before junior prom, her giving me the little stick after coming out of the bathroom at her parents' huge estate on Surmount Drive. My lips were raw from biting at dead skin while I waited shoulder leaning against the door frame.

We were both nervous, but I was better at hiding it. I had to be confident for her, that confident, unflustered rock she fell in love with. The test was negative. Since then we'd only taken two more. Not bad for students who'd attended a single sex education course unspooled through the groaning of a soccer coach. If I became a teen dad, my mother would've killed me. But the tests were always negative, always.

And then, like the childish fools we were, we would celebrate with sex, using protection rigidly for about two weeks before sinking back into our old dangerous habits. It was a miracle we graduated without a real incident. The fault was mine. I glamoured Markeya. She trusted me, and the more intense our bond became the more reckless I became with everything else.

Perhaps it was a form of selfish possession. An aggression against all precautions, barriers, or restraints. I didn't want to be careful if it meant having less of Markeya. I didn't accept any rules when it came to loving her like consequences didn't exist.

Now parked in front of Kayla McDaniels' electric green lawn, the beating of my blood muffled the sound of Markeya's shaky voice. Thoughts in my head were unknowable I stared down at the plastic pee stick in my hand. There was no fear, or worry, but also no elation or relief. I was suddenly in my own superhero backstory loop. As if the god of fatherhood had struck me with an invisible bolt and transmuted every chemical in my body. All I detected in my body was an instant overwhelming need to protect.

Never had there been the slightest expectation that I would feel this way. Not through all those negative tests, did I guess the change would be instantaneous.

But I didn't speak first. I had to know what she thought first.

"I can't—I can't be pregnant at this time in my life, Camden."

I turned to her, bemused. "What?"

She shook her head.

"Keya, what does that mean?"

She looked into her lap. "I'm not having it."

I waited a beat before I spoke, trying to be careful, trying to be considerate with my words. "How long have you known about this?"

"About two weeks," she said. The words echoed around me, and I struggled to contain a harsh reply. I swallowed it down but still I couldn't hide a bite of the pain when I spoke next.

"That's not fair," I told her, anger pulsing through my heart. And though I felt guilty after what she must have gone through for those two weeks alone, I couldn't help it. I was scared for the first time in my life.

"You've had time to make up your mind, but..." I stopped, licked my lips, unsure if I was about to say the right thing or was I speaking through a harried emotion. "It's mine too. And I haven't had time to think about what decision I'd like—"

Her eyes grew to the size of saucers as she turned to me. "You don't get to make that decision. Not for me."

"Jesus, Keya. Just wait a minute." my heart sank, "Please, just slow down and let's talk about this."

She flashed a fiery look at me, I'd never seen a look so challenging in her eyes before then. "I've made up my mind. You're going to be leaving in a few weeks. I'm supposed to start culinary school in a month. Who's going to help me with a baby?"

"I will." I struggled to form my words. I couldn't believe I was even saying it. What did a twenty year old Floridian wasp know about babies? But I was willing to say anything, do anything for a sliver of a chance. "Whatever you need I will make it happen, I swear. I'll leave the Marines."

She looked at me as if I'd offered to break my own arms. "What?"

I nodded, glad that for a moment, the suggestion had slowed her down. "I'll come back to Jacksonville and take that job at your dad's financial firm."

"I don't want you to do that. You couldn't even if you wanted to. The Marine Corps doesn't play backsies with flaky kids who knock up their girlfriends. You can't just leave the Marines," she breathed.

"If I did leave---."

"But you can't."

"If I did leave, would you reconsider?" I felt my insides boiling up with frustration. "Would you reconsider keeping my child and letting me take care of you here."

"It's not about the Marines, Cam." Markeya said. She dabbed the tears from her cheeks with her fingers. The white skirt she wore now sported tiny black wet streaks from her dripped mascara. "Plenty of girls find out they're pregnant right before the child's father is deployed. Its not about the Marines

"Do you want to get married?"

"Stop it," she said, her voice rising. "Stop trying to force me to do what I'm telling you I don't want to do. You don't want to marry me. "

My heart stopped at her words, "That's not true, Keya. I would marry you right now."

Markeya jumped out of the car and slammed the passenger door with all her might, bending down to scream at me through the open window. "You can't think for me, dammit!" A single tear splashed the doorjamb. I unbuckled my seat belt and hauled ass after her.

Markeya saw me coming and stopped on the sidewalk. She held her hand out to halt me. I stopped cold, "Why now?" she asked. "If you wanted to marry me then why wait until a monumental choice hangs in the balance."

"You're right, ok?" I said approaching her slowly, I feared for a moment she would fly away like a frightened bird. Instead, she fell quiet and still at my words.

The lazy swish-swish of the neighbors fanning sprinkling system was all the noise in existence for a moment. "You're right, I have crappy timing, sure. But Markeya, my feelings for you are real. I want to be your husband; I want our baby."

She shook her head slowly, her voice strained but resolute. "It's not about the timing or your feelings, Camden. It's about me, about what I want. I can't change my dreams and aspirations just because of our past or what's happening now."

A nasty tack of fright went through me when I repeated the words in my head. What's happening now considering the murders, the curfew, the lockdown, how sure could we be that we were thinking rationally. "I'm making the choice that's right for me. You can't decide what's right for me," Markeya finished, "You can't glamor me on this, Cam. Don't call me, don't come by. Not for a few days, I need some time alone. I have to do the right thing for the future. For both of us."

"Okay," my thoughts had gained approximately eight hundred pounds of weight, "If that's what you want. Just think about what I said. I mean it, Markeya, from the bottom of my heart. I love you."

I watched her leave, my own tears like boiling hot vapor blinding my eyes. I got into my car and punched the steering wheel until my hand ached and throbbed. The horn blared, loud enough to scare birds out of the trees, and I tore away from Kayla's house.

"You can't think for me, dammit."

When I'd gotten home, and after I'd calmed down, I called her.

***

I had to call and call until finally she answered. She muttered a few words, agreeing to sit down with me at some point during the week to figure things out---whatever that meant.

I could only hope we would figure things out. I could only hope to change her mind somehow. I wanted my baby; I wanted my family.

To distract myself, I picked up the game controller and isolated myself in the loft upstairs.

I had only been home from marine infantry training for two weeks, and had spent most of my time either catching up with friends, sleeping at Markeya's, or up in the loft at the Paratus estate house playing video games.

The next day was to be my last day of leave.

Afterward, I completed my infantry training where I'd learn the refined techniques in combat, I'd go to schooling for my preferred military occupational specialty: intelligence. I thought it would make Sergio proud, following him into the secret service or joining a special ops task force. After a few decades I could retire from service and open a custom home-building company. Building houses structures, even flipping fixer upper was an unscratchable itch that had tinged in me since childhood. I'd earned the dream of such a future through excruciating training and focus. And belief.

What were Markeya's beliefs? I knew her dreams quite well, but how much room did we have for each other in those dreams? Starting my military career meant forsaking her, and now forsaking my child. But sometimes I thought my parents, my family, only regarded me because I allowed their direction over my life and future.

Sure they loved Markeya but only because her father had been a state congressman and multi-business owner. He wasn't a head operative in the United States Secret Services like my father Chief Sergio Paratus, but Markeys family was a 'good' family. I was told I would pursue success, I would live a good life, serve and protect. And I nodded my head.

Admittedly, the predictability of maintaining the Paratus' respect and approval came with its own addictive ease. Their approval was both necessary and deterministic. No room for variation, interpretation, deviation. I didn't have to think about it. It was simple. I either stuck to their plan or lost them. To me, the cruelty of this dilemma was absurd but I had already made my choice. If Markeya stayed with me, if she chose to have a family with me, if she agreed to marry me, I would leave the Marines and do away with anything else that stood in my way. And I did mean anything that stood in my way.

I had pulled out the test to study the little red lines just when my mother stomped up the stairs to the loft, sobbing on the phone, her voice shrill with fear. I quickly stuffed the little white stick below my waistband.

"Mom, what the heck are you crying about?" I asked, trying to cover my own alarm.

She seemed deaf to my voice. But her words flashed me with something creeping and slimy.

I suddenly felt a cold breath trace over my scalp. I'd never seen such a look in her eyes. I'd never seen any woman look the way my mother looked at me just then. I stood slowly "What's going on?" I said.

"I have Sergio on the phone, he's leaving Washington, he's coming to get us." Giovanna's voice slurred, stuttered.

She picked up the television remote, and my game screen flickered to a news channel. I peered at the footage rolling beside the anchorman's head. What I saw stunned me into silence.

It can't be, I thought, but I was seeing it. Vampires aren't real, they're fictitious creatures, villains in Halloween films, the figurative language a cynic would use to describe their co-worker. Some folklorist YouTube channels erred in calling vampires 'cryptids. They didn't quite fit that category, Markeya told me, unless you accounted for the lack of scientific evidence that any species categorized by cryptozoology existed.

I thought I was crazy, of course. But there they were, frantic on Local Jax News Channel 9. A helicopter provided a bird's eye view of the moving, unbroken crowd.

There were two crowds actually. One made of armored enforcers,--- swat? National Guard? And one marching in formation like an army, except the parties of this crowd wore an array of clothing belonging to anything but a military. Grey twill skirts, knitted pants, football jerseys, ruffled floral dresses, tunics, khaki shorts, oversized hoodies, distressed jeans, converse sneakers, leather oxford, nurses shoes. I saw Ponytails, extensions, braided dreads, highlights and lowlights, bald heads. What I didn't was the jostle of panic, the scuttling ant colony most footage depicted from the same vantage point. Usually attack footage, featured people fleeing the wreckage, choking on the smoke, wriggling survivors from beneath piles of shrapnel.

But this crowd of civilians plunged down Town Center Hillston Avenue. Turning the heads of the curious patrons who'd been at the coffee shops and delicatessens who'd been enjoying a coffee break or nice sandwich and were now watching in its perfect grid down the avenue.

By the time they came in direct contact with armor-clad riot police, they were leaping. Their hands were ripping, their teeth biting.

I felt Giovanna shrink back with a deep hiss of horror next to me.

I remembered the tremors in my veins. "What the hell is this?"

We had been waiting to hear for weeks about the D.C. Mayor's cause of death—the man found poolside, drained of every drop of blood. What was strange, besides the fact that nobody could have snuck past the security surrounding the mansion, was how they found D.C. Mayor Richardson.

In a twisted heap on the pool deck, his neck ripped open. Stiff wide-eyed despair frozen across his contorted face. His eyes stared at the overhead conifer trees.

Surrounding his body, police found five mason jars—jars kindergarteners use for making crafts—filled to their lids with dark burgundy blood. The police had the blood tested and confirmed it belonged to the D.C. Mayor. The case became a national spectacle. What kind of killer can drain a person's blood and preserve it in mason jars? And why?

Every news station broadcasted details of this heinous and confusing crime scene. Some speculated there was a maniac on the loose—maybe an elite spy gone insane—but then the event repeated itself 1,000 miles away in Florida, my home state.

"Soon the killers graduated to governors and senators, and in weeks, entire nations were thrown into chaos as this surreal nightmare rapidly spread throughout the country and now internationally." The anchorwomnn's voice radiated over the news footage "Nations have lost local and federal leaders. Panic and crowds of violent assailants have diverged on citizens and law enforcement as whomever or whatever this killer is continues to blaze a path of destruction through leadership from all corners of the world."

My eyes danced over the screens, viewing a rapid montage of cities overrun. Hordes of people crowding the street in front of the White House, people on the Las Vegas Strip, people shouting, fighting and marching on embassy grounds, calling for....

I paused, hitching a breath, shuddering. I thought I saw a man take a hulking bite out of a police officer.

I squinted, trying to read some of the signs, trying to decipher the jumbled clip. "What is happening— they're killing members of the National Guard, with bare hands?"

"I-I don't know." Giovanna put down her champagne flute. That day she had decided to throw on a pale pink pajama set—one of her favorites—but she didn't even flinch when the glass tilted and dripped on the silk pants.

Finally, the news camera focused long enough that I could see one of the women clearly in frame. Her jaws clamped down on the shoulder of a servicewoman, who screamed soundless agony. The attacker had the eyes of a mad lioness. Vicious distortion in her brow, a fury unfamiliar to me, and there was something else about her, something that couldn't be accepted by a rational-thinking person. And I didn't accept it, until she unlatched from the slumped servicewoman, and bared her hateful grin at the camera.

Her mouth dripped fresh blood. She swiped her long red tongue across a set of gleaming white fangs.

***

Jacksonville International Airport- Second Floor Haskell Gallery Mens' RestRoom

My eye watched blood creep like a spider under the door gap, pooling a few feet away from my face.

Two voices sounded off in my head. They spoke over one another.

God, save me.

Fuck, I'm thirsty.

Had someone broken me in half and stitched me back together? Had the two parts of that stitched-together person ceased to agree with its opposite half. Was I of two minds now? Forever?

I moved my eyeball to the side, where I'd heard a scream tear through the walls that enclosed me. I pictured where in the building the scream could've come from, and whether or not it would be the last scream I should've expected to hear again. And then the barely detected agony in my belly became a loud roar of gnawing. It racked through me. I pressed my face into the floor, tucked my chin to my chest and gritted. Plastic laminate stalks shrank before me. The concave mouth of the porcelain urinal seemed to deepen under the lights.

The most bedeviling stretch of the pain unlocked itself like vice grip and I expelled voice and breath in on heave. The wailing outside of the restroom ceased, and my own grated rasping breath was all I could hear. I was sober. Not even wailing though I should've been. The droning cramp I felt in my stomach was half-animal. When it stopped and became a throb, the type of throb that promises a new wave, I rolled flat on my back as if dropped from the sky after an alien abduction. But worse was to come.

I didn't know who I was for far too long. What was my name?

Where was I?

On a floor. Not in my house. The floor was hard, cold. The sensation gave me the same feelings you get when you wake up in a hotel, when you maybe panic for a minute realizing you're not in your own bedroom. That happened to me a lot when I was little... but this was no cozy, sexy little Airbnb in the south of Florida. I had woken up in hell.

A blinding halogen light scored my eyes, a ghostly orb unblinking and aggressive. Assaulting. I wanted to punch it to raining shards.

Bastard.

I'd woken up in hell. Hell itself. I heard the screams start up again, barely reaching my ears but somehow also inside my head. Rolling around like an outlaw tinball down a vortex simulator.

I didn't want to hear people dying but what could I do? Not even able to mentally find my fingers to plug my ears. I could only lay prone on the hard floor listening to pipes gurgling.

A toilet, I thought.

I was in hell. I knew hell. At least I thought I had. I did after all survive the week of the crucible at Marine boot camp, should've been called Hell, I guess. Worst fucking week of my life until now. Because now I was deaf from the screams, and gunfire I thought. The gunfire. I tensed, dizzy and nauseous, remembering then that I had shot a gun. How I knew I didn't know.

And I was bleeding and—

Fuck. The pain.

My stomach twisted and the agony of it, the memory of the gunfire, the regurgitated screams, jolted my body awake. I launched up, and curled into myself, my intestines squeezed like I'd guzzled a full gallon of gasoline. Bubbling fizzing.

I vomited like something out of the exorcism, throwing up red bile. Mom's spaghetti. I almost smile because I knew I'd gone fucking crazy.

Obviously.

Why else had the thought that I'd thrown up blood come to mind?

I wiped my mouth staring at the thunder spreading like spilled syrup on the floor. I was in some sort of devastated trance, using logic to wrestle with reality.

It's not blood, genius. Of course it's not.

It was Giovanna's fancy spaghetti, ---lobster and shrimp stirred in tomato cream sauce. The chefs had stopped coming to the estate. The house staff had all quit because of the... murders. Giovanna took over dinnertime but skill escaped her efforts as much as enthusiasm suffused them.

But it smells like blood, that other voice piped in.

I wiped my mouth again and the sleeve of my white shirt came away dark red.

But there was something else on the fabric too. I stared carefully. There was a little brush of something bright rubescent in color starting right above my elbow. Something still deeply wet and splotched. Fresh blood. I scanned the length of my sleeve until right below my collar, where my throat was. And then I realized, the entire length of my neck, on the right side, down to my shoulder was drenched in the stuff.

Had someone cut my throat? I squeezed my neck hunting for an open wound. Memories of the gory chaos in the airport came in white flashes. My Adam's apple lept when I touched, feeling my own skin as if some part of me expected to find a squelching gaping hole there instead of my intact jugular. But there was nothing, save for a sandy stubble and tacky flaking blood.

I was in one piece but not quite whole.

Pain lanced through my body again. I pulled myself up using the wall, leaving streaked fingerprints on the white brick. Dizzy and nearly slipping in the puke under my black sneakers, I planted my back on the wall, exhaling through my teeth. The pain in my belly was hollow but mind numbing. I fought through it and lifted my shirt to check for gunshot or stab wounds.

To my surprise, there were none. What I did see was much more terrifying. Flares of dark bruises spider-legged across my ribcage and sternum. Not only that, but something was pulsated inside me. The flesh covering the area of my pancreas should've been flexed, depressed then crawled like something trying to break out from within.

What does internal bleeding look like?

Can it be seen through skin? Do ruptured organs pulse?

I rushed to the bathroom sink, thinking, hoping that seeing the contusions from the other side of my vantage point could make them appear clearer. I squinted the light away, inspecting the marks, the thin broken vein-like patterns. The curved plain of muscle stretched. My stomach was more purple with splotches of black than ivory white. I lowered the shirt and stared at my face. And the moment I paid attention to the reflection, I noticed something astounding.

I squeeze my eyes shut at the face peering wide-eyed at me. Dipping my hands in the running water, I leaned down and scrubbed the blood from my face until the water ran clear. Then I inspected my reflection again.

What I saw in the smeared glass had to be a hallucination. It appeared, for a moment, that my teeth had changed.

I believed in medical miracles; I'd seen wondrous acts of human feat. I had read many editions of the Guinness book of records and watched many disturbing YouTube videos. But never had I heard of human teeth changing, --- growing--- from square and stump, to long and sharp.

I fumbled away from the sink, tripping over my feet, the room spun.

"This isn't real." I groaned, plaintively to myself. To whom was I complaining? Who could hear me demanding a sense out of what was senseless.

And then as if in answer, an ear-splitting knock resounded on the door.

I swung the door open and fell out into a long hallway. My surroundings registered, the state of Jacksonville International Airport dawned on me. And all at once, I died inside.

Everything came storming back. I was in the airport because we'd been fleeing the country. Mom, dad and me, we'd been standing in line to board a plane. I'd been seconds from slipping away, determined to skirt the trip and find Markeya, when...something had happened. And that something had left turmoil in its wake

Nausea rolled up to my stomach and I whited out for a second.

The aftermath, the disarray, the soaked carpet and splashed walls surrounding me brought the prior carnage roaring to the present. The memories of teeth breaking skin, bones crunching on top of me as I crushed, slammed and strangled as many of the — things as I could.

People were dead. People were in pieces. They'd been hoping to catch a flight or waiting out a layover and now they were in pieces scattered around the second floor like Mega Bloks.

And not only were the people around me dead, but it seemed the whole world had expired. The most painful of silences met my chaotic breath. Blood, dank and foul, drenched and burned my nostrils. I stepped out onto the carpet and felt it squelch under my shoe. Blood striped the endless walls which traveled north of me, headed for a collection of elevators.

I looked down. Someone's foot, still attached to a leg and nothing more, was jammed between the railings of the second floor balcony like a string bean in the prongs of a fork.

Like mixed jigsaw pieces the parts were everywhere. Arms attached to hands but not attached to shoulders. I felt the lining peel from my stomach but there was nothing to eject any more.

Before I took another step, he came around the corner where the elevators should've connected all these dead people to different floors. He sauntered toward me as if he'd been waiting for an appointment.

Sergio Paratus, my father, secret service. The vampire.

Yes, I remembered now. How his eyes turned that awful infrared amber. He was the cause, he was part of it, and he'd dragged me into it with him.

I grabbed the base of my neck. The flesh there was as hot as burning coals on a grill. The pads of my finger came away tacky. There should've been a jagged wound somewhere. I remembered him fucking biting through my throat.

"Camden," he said in one low note.

And as he stood there straight as a pin, in a tailored suit, he looked as if it had never happened. At least his expression said so. The rest of him told a different, horrifying story. In his arms, Sergio Paratus clutched the wrist of a broken human body. A young raven-haired woman, in yoga pants and purple blouse. One breast exposed, neck dripping on the carpet.

How wetness dripped down my cheek. Heartache cut me to the bone.

Sergio's hair was mussed, his dress shirt untucked, his lips were smiling.

My mother was nowhere to be found. Instead, I counted one, two and three more figures that looked like him. Two appeared from the alcove of elevators, one meandering up the downed escalator on the right of me. I was hemmed in by fangs tailored suits.

My father leaned down, and jerked the dazed woman's wrist to his lips and bit down. Slurping like a sloppy kid enjoying soup.

"Where's Giovanna?" I whispered.

Sergio and the vampires who'd come so close I smelled nothing but tobacco even over the saturated blood, looked at me. My father dropped the corpse dead on the carpeted floor.

Sergio clapped his hands together, blood casted off when he did so. He stepped over the woman's dead body. I stepped back. My thoughts were chaotic, wondering what I should do. Should I make a citizen's arrest of all of them?

"You bit me." I said hesitantly as Sergio smiled and his friends chuckled. Who were these people? I couldn't recall ever meeting them before, despite thinking I had met most of my dad's friends. Was this even my father?

Sergio introduced them one by one- Lamarc, Kenneth, and Reginald - to me, referring to me as his only son. My scalp prickled with unease as all three men turned their attention towards me while my alleged father continued to stare at me. He held out his hand as if expecting me to take it, but my feet remained rooted in place.

"Who was that?" I managed to choke out eventually, nodding towards the crumpled dead woman on the airport carpet. "What was her name? Why--- why?"

Sergio looked confused for a moment before glancing behind him at the corpse. "How would I know that?" he asked dismissively.

And that was it. I had lost it. Synapses snapped, vocal cords shriveled, lungs ceased taking in air. I laughed frosted over with panic. Giving in fully to it. Letting it take me below the carpet, below the first floor below the Earth's crust.

"Come here, Camden," he continued impatiently. "Let's go home. We need to talk before you are fully endowed."

"It will be slow...painful," Lamarc chimed in ominously.

"Perhaps you should incubate him for a few years," suggested Reginald.

"Overkill," Kenneth interjected, eyeing me up and down appraisingly. "I agree with Ken, six months if he's got enough of your stock should be more than enough,"

Sergio concluded, "Men, I think I know what is best for my son." He smiled a grin of all fangs, and that's when I lost sight of everything.

***

My eyes snapped open. Reality, even if invisible, snapped back into shape. Consciousness mushroomed. My escape from the afterlife, as in the cases of others, came with a lesson. If called, I could reiterate only a thread of it. Indeed, total darkness and absolute nothingness were too different species. I had escaped the nothing of unreality, and believed the manner in which I was sent to that unraveled place, my afterlife, had been blacker than the darkest of nights.

Entrenched by the impossible wrongness of betrayal the mind creates pitfalls, and those pitfalls cored to my soul. There was nothing to grab onto there, no rope to entwine with my tired and pursuing fingers, no way to pull my lame body from the swallowing jowls of eternal nothing. I simply stopped. Stopped. Then eternity hawked me out again.

Out I returned into total darkness. That was how I could tell the difference. I felt it. A dark space in front of me, behind me, on each side. Locked in some cold dark chamber.

I wouldn't even attempt to adjust my pin straight, arms-to-the-side position. I knew I couldn't move. The cold dewy smell of metal wafted too close to my face. A thorough exhale caused my shoulders and elbows to bump into the walls. Flexing the balls of my feet brought my skin in contact with the floor of this place. The crown of my head pushed against a hard ceiling which couldn't comfortably accommodate my height.

I'm buried, the harried voice that had woken me in the airport returned. I'm buried underground. The attack at the airport, I died in it. Or at least my family thought I had died and had arranged my funeral. I was six feet in the ground but not dead.

Then the other voice answered, the one I knew I truly owned, the one that hadn't grown out of the irrationality of all I'd seen the past few days but had been with me since the day I could think. That part of me still believed it all had been a dream. The vampires, my father's fangs, the airport bathroom.

Well I'll have to break out, won't I? It said, Somehow. Some fucking how. And if I do manage to break out, I'll do my level best to never remind my family of this horrible mistake they had made.

But how do I get out? I thought, but before the answer came to me, those thoughts were snapped off.

A flower bud of pain grew at my navel like petals of a ravenous plant closed up in sepals. My rapid breath involuntarily attempted to erode the knot. My diaphragm kicked on its own. But breathing did nothing. Without arms I could move there was not even hope of kneading loose the contracted ball of needles. The bud swelled. The petals inside begin to grow and expand, pushing against the sepals. The sepals slowly started to separate and peel back as the petals grew larger.

I was howling, I realized. A spicy, powdery vibration coated my teeth and tongue like turmeric. The bones in my ears were rattling. The painful little petals grew. Unfolding heat through my body in the dark, in this cramped closed space. This tomb. The explosion like puffy flowers, numerous and layered, fully expanded and separated my senses from the darkness. Like dying all over again, this peak was both beautiful and permanent, displaying vibrant colors in intricate swimming arrangements. I could see suddenly. I saw everything in its stark reality.

With this new vision came something so stunningly obvious, something so frank and inescapable my acceptance of it was near instinctual and completely hopeless. I stopped groaning in agony altogether. The pain cooled only a fraction but I went utterly still. Bringing the full bloom of realization to its final fruition.

This scourge of pain was thirst. Phenomenal, extraordinary, preternatural thirst

I could see in the dark now. I could sense and taste the texture of the dark. Scaly, crumbly, like the peeling bark of the river birch. I was twelve in the boys scouts when I learned to identify one of those towering trees. It was Panama City's Econfina Creek where scoutmaster Mr. Johnson, with his graying beard, led us on a hike through Pine Log State Forest. He showed us trees and plants because to his bafflement, the scurrying creatures down to the tiniest buzzing flea, became preternaturally still when we entered the woods in line like a hunting party. That was the word he used to describe the silence 'preternatural.' And I swore he looked at me when he said it. I swore. .

The memory brought the howling pain to a light stutter. Bit by bit, my lungs relaxed, my pulse rocked slower. I still would've jumped from a cliff had I stood before one.

Where the fuck are you, just focus on that.

A great question if one ever did exist, since as far as I knew funeral homes didn't bury the dead in metal coffins.

A red blinking light flickered awake, shining straight into my skull. In its glow, I saw cream-colored cushioning and metal bolts stapled into a concave wall above me. I ran my hands over the surface. A chemical stench wafted from the walls like Windex and plastic. That was all the air held. Not a single sound inside or a single echo outside.

I had been entombed, but not in a graveyard.

It was obvious that I was not the one who put me in here, but I remembered nothing beyond the airport and Sergio's friends. I remembered only the bodies, the blood, the death. The memories following had been wiped out.

Were those memories real, were they? What if my senses had encoded the events incorrectly? Perhaps I hadn't heard screams but planes accelerating. I might not have smelled blood but rare meat from the food court. I hadn't looked in the mirror and saw sharp teeth stretching from my pink gums but a broken tooth. Had I gotten into a scuffle at the boarding gate and taken a chair to the head? Or if there had been an explosion, or a chemical attack, might not the resulting injury affect brain function? Especially memory retrieval?

Using every muscle I had, I pounded myself against the metal casing, making all the racket I could, making the metal groan. The only time I stopped was to listen for footsteps or voices on the other side. None came. Nothing but complete silence met my ears.

I ignored the omen of what that meant, the prospect of spending eternity in the darkness, and I pounded harder, someone— somewhere had to fucking hear me. After an eternity passed with no release, fury finally took hold of me.

I fought the restraints with the same blazing mad violence one turns on innocent bystanders in lieu of their true enemy. And I was pleading silently as the memories of the airport bathroom swarmed back with devouring ferocity.

It was real, it was.

The vampires, the massacre. My father turning to me with those red, glinting eyes, those sharp white fangs.

I had seen my own fangs in the dark bathroom mirror. I'd remembered seeing the face, which was not my own, staring at me with its stunned expression, pale as egg white, and struck through with shocking blue veins. And there were blood stains on my collar, I'd touched the fabric, and my fingers had come back sopping wet. I remember ripping myself away in fear. Moving with me, the sounds of laughter and the faint squeaks of shoes touching the airport tile had seeped into bathroom——

The metal lid swung open; I squinted in sudden, blinding light. As my eyes adjusted painfully, I saw her. Giovanna, my mother - wearing a snakish smile.

Her fangs, pearly and white, glistened as she spoke. "Rise and shine, sleeping beauty."

***

Giovanna carefully set the glass of blood in front of me. I recoiled at the sight of it but something in my throat shifted. I had never drunk blood in my life. Who has? Even when I'd accidentally bitten my cheek too hard, I had involuntarily spat out the coppery-flavored saliva. My mind refused to accept this.

I was in my own home, but there was an eerie unfamiliarity to the large dining room. The fine tablecloth was gone, the place settings missing. The room felt enormously empty yet crowded with the pulsing anticipation of my family.

Or were they my family anymore?

Were they ever?

I had expected to one day leave the Paratus estate to start a family of my own. Protect, provide, play silly games with kids who had missing teeth and new skin. I would put away money in a college fund, envision horrible scenarios before their first day of school, thank my wife every anniversary for staying with me. From the left, Giovanna glared at me as if she saw the whole world flash in my eyes.

Sergio, with his stern hard glare, waited opposite his wife, one arm on the table so he could lean a little further toward me. His early flippancy, if I had been remembering the airport correctly, had dissolved. He watched my frozen figure like a cinema buff watches an old silent film. His hair was combed but still wet from a shower. Giovanna had hurried him into the dining room from the master room after lowering me unsteadily into one of the chairs.

Before me, a long swathe of thick mustard-colored fabric, which Markeya would've called Chenille, because of the 'piles', covered the bay window of the adjoined breakfast nook. I bet all the windows had been covered. The thousands of square feet stretched out around me hung in taupe and stone gray. Every bit of the Paratus estate had become a dark mausoleum, the limestone, the Venetian plaster, the crown molding, the wrought iron and leather accents.

Giovanna stood, tred along the hard floors, her steps made no sounds, her silk pajamas gleamed and I didn't know why but something in me flinched when she moved toward me. She moved too fast to be my mother, too fluidly like a sylph or some other elemental being.

I grew up watching her hop around clutching one foot after stubbing her toe on the furniture, or catching her in my arms before she tumbled down the front steps of the estate in the rain. I'd always thought myself an athlete and she an indulged, feathery artist. Giovanna to my eyes had always been a genius, a spy, the most beautiful, difficult, frank and just woman in the world. But I feel the way she floats to stand beside me, and think was it all a lie? Had that clumsiness and everything else been pretense of hers all along?

"Family traditions are a little different for us than for humans, Camden," she said. "And in some ways they are much the same. Unalike your average human, vampires transcend the very concept of time itself. For some of us, time only exists in the mind. Do you know what that feels like? Time can be extinguished if one isn't careful. With a single rational thought we can become untethered. That means, much as it is in human society but far more significantly, traditions are all that anchors us to where we are meant to be. We must keep our traditions, we must hold them sacred or perish existentially. That fact is eventual, darling. Do you understand?"

Her hand closed carefully on my shoulder, the sharp burgundy-painted nails looked like velvet on the end of her snow-white fingers. She pulled the crimson-filled glass closer to me.

Sergio glanced up at her, shifting in his seat as if enthralled to know what I would do, how she would manipulate me. As if the whole world hinged on the success of the deceptively chatty, and once idiosyncratic woman who birthed me but who was now, I believed threatening me.

"Some things are more important than traditions, and would lead to death should we attempt to negotiate them. This fact, my love, is immediate." Giovanna went on. The glass of blood blurred before my eyes. The wooden arms of the dining chair letting of whistling creak as my grip tightened.

You have a choice, my inner voice slinked along the crevices of silence. It may not seem that way in the least but you do. All pretense of civility has passed, and the consequences for your integrity are sure to be abominable but you still make the decision yourself. They could not force me in a million years to drink the blood. I would out-fight them, out-monster them if they tried. But they didn't need to force anything, that was the truth we all understood.

 I tried to suppress it.

"I am not---," I meant to protest with verve and stalwart vigor, but the act of moving my lips dampened my resolve to keep away from the blood. I had to finish the rest of the objection in my mind. I am not a vampire. I'm not a vampire. It felt good, the mantra, the lie but I couldn't deny the twisting thought lurking beneath my consciousness like a predator, hungry and drooling. The horrible truth. I wanted the blood. Badly. I wished to take it from the table, bring it to my lips, guzzle it down, break the cup in my hand. My new teeth, pointed, polished bone. They buzzed behind my lips.

I met my father's gaze. Those eyes swam with a whole new light. And that light was sharp, cutting, like glass knives slicing through me. He stood and I followed his path until he stood behind me.

I imagined he had taken Giovanna around the waist and pulled her snug into his ribs as he always would when they stood together. A chill ran cold down my spine as I felt Sergio's cold fingers close around my skull.

"Drink, Camden," he said, his voice like distant thunder. "If you don't, the thirst will take you-- kill you."

I frowned at the glass. Someone's blood cells floated microscopically in there. Billions upon billions upon billions. Where had they gotten the blood? Who did the blood belong to? A dead person? A child? Tears formed at the corners of my eyes. I looked at my hands on the table, nails sharper and whiter than I remembered them.

"Do you understand, Camden, you must drink," he repeated.

"I'd rather die," I whispered.

"My son is not going to die." Giovanna's tone croaked. I'd never heard her sound so throttled. "We will shove a tube down your throat first," she promised.

I had never experienced such anguish and rage towards my own mother. She had always been the center of my universe. She mended my first broken heart with a poem from one of her favorite books. She forced an adroitness for cradling the bow of a cello into my fingers. Her name was tattooed on my shoulder. I loved her more than life itself. But the fear for another consumed me.

Why not just leave, or subdue them both?

My legs didn't work. Nothing worked, not even my heart. I'd believed important connections between my brain and nervous system needed rebooting since the metal coffin.

"Camden, your mother is right, we will not let you. You will drink or be made to drink." Sergio pushed the glass ever closer to my trembling hands. "Please son. Bring it to your lips, your instincts will do the rest."

I licked my lips, and incredulous tears finally came. One drop fell from my chin into the glass and rippled in the dark red liquid. I didn't try to wipe it. I licked my lips and tasted its salty remnant.

Sergio clenched his fists to his side. "I beg you. We are your family Camden, you don't have to be a soldier right now. Trust us, have we ever allowed harm to come to you?"

I felt the heat of my anger rise. I looked at my father, then my mother. "Both of you, you're both fucking sick."

Sergio gave a heavy sigh and stood straight, towering over me. With sickening clarity, I realized the syringe in his hand was intended for me. Before I could react, he grasped me firmly, then the stab of a needle plunged into my neck.

The darkness was crushing, suffocating until I was nothing but broken pieces of the person I once was.

I wasn't going to wake up this time and I did the torture would be never-ending

I clung to the memory of Markeya like a lifeline in my drug-induced nightmare. Her golden skin, golden hair, golden eyes. Like sunlight piercing the abyss. I reached out to her with all of my might, screaming her name as the shadows closed in around me with ripping claws and sharp teeth. With every passing second, her face became more and more distant until the darkness completely swallowed me and all that remained was an unbearable loneliness.

In a clinging sweat, I jolted awake. The scent of damp and mildew hung in the air. I noticed this as the same stench since the airport. The damp, the stink, no matter where I went. It had even followed me in the realm of my nightmares. I blinked, letting my eyes adjust to the scene around me.

Before I fully recognized the room the panic had already set in. I was strapped down to a chair I didn't recognize, in some forgotten corner of my family basement. Most of the three thousand square-foot space drowned beneath stacks of ancient computer equipment and medical machines. Slatted utility shelves smothered in storage boxes glutted the room and I saw a spider the size of my thumb creep up the wall behind the one closest to me.

I'd visited the basement before, years ago as a ten-year-old searching for treasure—but it hadn't looked anything like this. Dread crept up my chest. I wrestled against the bindings in the dim, windowless room, feeling not only trapped but entombed in the cavernous basement.

No sound except my own labored breathing broke the eerie silence. I filled up that silence even more with a shout. Calling for Sergio, Giovanna, knowing I'd receive no reply. I went on bellowing anyway with all the strength in my body.

The floor could've opened and swallowed me, I'd been thinking, and no one would hear it.

But then the oppressive weight of another--- someone who stood just behind me---pressed down on my awareness like an iron fist. All at one I went quiet, and extremely still. I used to think the basement was haunted. These creative thoughts began after I'd watched the movie House on Haunted Hill. I always thought our house resembled the mansion in that film but surely that was ridiculous.

Or was it? Because apparently, a man could drink the blood of another while not only avoiding disease but gaining nutritional benefits. Surely, our basement could harbor a ghost.

A footstep sent my heart rate to heaven. I strained against the metal cuffs locking my wrists to the chair.

Each muscle in my body ached from my efforts, but the struggle was no use.

"Absolutely impenetrable steel," The basement door whined as it swung open. A chute of light punctured the gloom from the staircase across from me. Sergo appeared in the door frame. "And of course I injected you with a combination of liquid silver and ultraviolet. I'm so sorry about this, son," he said, "You've left us no choice." I noticed he was dressed in joggers and barefooted. Wrapped up for a cozy night at home on any regular evening in the suburbs.

I felt a strange squeeze of sadness as his eyes led the way down the creaking stairs. His thudding assured footfalls the only sound amidst the oppressive silence. He held some wad of grotesque equipment in his arms.

Somehow while the tubes and clamps meant nothing to my eyes, an inner knowing warned the twisting guts below my stomach of the wickedness ahead. Something was wrong, besides being tied to a chair in a dank basement. Something unforgivably horrible hung in the air, the same awful crush of dejection you'd feel finding a fingernail in a bowl of soup swam up in my mind.

As my father stepped toward me, I wanted to leave more than I wanted my next breath. I wanted to leave more than I wanted to live.

"What are you doing?" I asked, To my own ears, I sounded authoritative and confident, like I had spent months getting my ass handed to me in U.S Marine Corps boot camp. Like every vestige of fear had been strategically and thoroughly carved out of me by the full might of the American military. All that confidence and anger went away once I recognized the equipment gripped in his hands.

Florida was a state prone to natural disasters, and Sergio believed in staying ready for the unexpected. In the event of a major disaster disrupting the availability of food or causing a nasty injury necessitating dire measures, an enteral feeding kit would be invaluable.

"Let me out of this fucking chair." I roared, my voice shaking the foundations of the house. Suddenly, hands landed on my shoulders from behind. The basement ghost from my twelve year old mind, except its grip was as solid and ice cold as that of a statue.

Giovanna.

Her grip was stronger than any normal person's despite her small frame. She whispered softly and sorrowfully, trying to gull me to a level of calm. "Hold still my love, it ends quicker that way." But I could hear the underlying tremble in her voice.

***

Giovanna, from a cushioned accent chair, regaled me with tales of my vampire forefathers. My mind dwelled elsewhere, turning again and again to Markeya and the fateful day we said goodbye. Through the physical pain, the edges of the memory shimmered and hazed but from through the mental anguish I managed to recall pursuing her down the sidewalk after she'd jumped out of my care.

I remembered her hair flinging over one shoulder as she rounded on me, yelling. Then the single tear pricking her left eye had turned her brown iris black.

"Camden," Giovanna pulled me out of the scene. I gripped the scuffed wooden chair, causing the shackles to dig deeper into my wrist. My mouth and esophagus stung from the coarse tubing Sergio had jammed down my throat.

I want to fall off the face of the Earth. I want to burn down the house with all of us inside.

"Are you listening?" Giovanna asked in a small voice, peeking at me over the top of an open leather journal, eyes rimmed in dark mascara. "These histories are very important. Insight into who you are lies between these pages, no vampire on Earth had access---."

"Too late for fucking insight don't you think?" It hurt to speak. Like choking down nails. A headache vised my skull like a cable clamp, and I burned from the slow-healing bruise on my throat. I had never felt such pain from such small, invisible places. Having been forced to ingest blood (whose blood? Whose?) made all those sensations stronger.

Sergio had explained it to me a minute before he left Giovanna and I below, in the dark basement. After assuring I wouldn't puke up all of his hard work of course, he elucidated, "You'll feel more than you've ever felt now that you've taken blood for the first time," he had said like a doctor giving a rushed prognosis "And as a pureblood, you'll feel more than you ever could've had you been human." His words devoured my thoughts like a spiked parasite and I shuddered. As a pureblood, I knew what that meant, anyone with half a brain would've known.

I wasn't a human, never had been, I'd lived a lie all nineteen years of my life.

I remembered Serio glancing at Giovanna who'd been meticulously wiping the spilled blood from my face. "Be careful for the next few hours," he told her. "He might suffer a surge and break his own arms to get out of those restraints."

"They'll hold him? You're sure?" she had asked in return. I could tell from the sound of her voice she was taking pains to keep any concern out of her tone.

Endlessly patient when it came to Giovanna, Sergio smiled. "They're impenetrable," he emphasized. "Even for one of us. He isn't going anywhere."

Then he left, and we'd been waiting in the basement for his return ever since. A couple of times Giovanna had gone upstairs to bring down another novel or a glass of wine. But for the most part we glared at each other. We listened to the sounds of her airy Renaissance era Italian as she read from the crumbling journal. She had gossipy ancestors as most of the entries written by Isabella Conti, Marchioness of Capua, recounted court intrigue and outrageous scandals in the Kingdom of Naples.

"See, here is where the Duchess of Amalfi mistakes Alessandro di Napoli for another noble lady," Giovanna was giddy at this point, in her silk white pajamas, both feet hiked up in the dining chair she'd brought from downstairs. She sipped her wine again and held the book higher. "Because, you know, he was adorned extravagantly in a peacock costume for the masque---" She stopped short, lowered the book, unbelievably checking whether I was listening again.

I wasn't. I was staring at the pocket knife Sergio had left on a dusty end table against the left wall. And I was picturing Markeya in my arms. I wondered if she was still alive. Did she escape before it was too late? Was she alone? Worse yet, was she or was she not pregnant?

The pee stick was back at the boarding gate, most likely crushed and blood splattered. But the two red lines I'd seen on the test screen stayed with me.

Even when I'd woken in the airport, even inside that horrid metal chamber while I was begging to be let go. Those two little red lines gripped my mind as snug as a back-stitch.

Two lines meant positive, one meant negative. That was all Markeya ever told me about pregnancy tests. That and the technology wasn't perfect, which I could've surmised on my own about all technology. Maybe she wasn't pregnant. A pang of hope clutched my stomach as I thought of it.

The last two times she'd taken one, she had said something about false positives. False negatives. Yes, she'd mentioned a fear of false negatives, though she assured us both the chance of such a thing happening was as slim as finding a four-leaf clover in a wildflower meadow.

Still, I remembered thinking what was the point of shelling out 20 dollars a box for results you couldn't trust? And Markeya had said something that made me laugh so hard and deliciously, I struggled to breathe.

Something about paying for the fantasy, as with a psychic hotline where you pay to hear the lie you want to hear. In our idiot teenage case, it made sense. We would've paid someone to tell us we'd dodged the well-deserved bullet of premature pregnancy, even if it wasn't true. But it had been a true negative again and again. Until it wasn't a negative at all.

I nearly smiled at the memory. Sitting in that car and seeing the second line charted by the first, likely an exact centimeter apart. Double trouble, I had thought after the white-hot panic and sheer naked joy,---- two emotions which had jammed themselves in me tangled around each other,----finally settled down. But the memory of it quickly grew into a thick, slimy mold. Markeya was out there all alone. And the odds of a false pregnancy were 'four-leaf clover slim.' If she was alive, then she would be carrying my baby unprotected and without me.

Giovanna's voice faded away.

"I want to be let out of this chair, out of this house." I spoke.

"I know that Camden, but I can not free you from the chair. I made Sergio a promise. I never break my promises to my husband," she set her crystal wine glass down, like a grade school teacher who's just set a disruptive student straight and leafed through the journal. "I'm trying to get through the story of Kai, don't you want to know a little more about your heritage?"

I sighed deeply, "I don't want to have to hurt you."

Giovanna shut the red book and flashed her eyes at me. "What was that?"

I didn't know how to respond. I guessed those words had come from a place that was desperate, a place that meant every syllable.

"It's extremely disrespectful to interrupt me when I'm educating you about Kai, Camden. Most purebloods pay college tuition to learn about the history of the First and don't ever get close to this kind of authenticity," she wagged the journal violently in my face.

"You're insane. You both are." I took a moment to compose myself. "The streets are full of people, but they are not the same people we once knew, are they? They're like you, right? Killers. You, and him?" I nodded toward the basement door meaning Sergio.

"We are those killers, Camden. We've always been. Now you know."

Closing the journal and setting the book aside, she tilted her head at me. For exactly one breath, I felt like Little Red Riding Hood peering into the glittering eyes of the wolf. "The world is ours now Camden. You'll have to help rebuild it in our image. Get on with this shock of yours quickly. I did and you're of my stock."

Her last sentence, uttered with a roll of her eyes, went through me and triggered something hostile and explosive. She had appeared terrified in the upstairs loft, the warble of fear in her voice as she hammered Sergio with questions over the phone had totally convinced me of that fact. They were watching the world end together, the news story was like a horror show. I hadn't seen long pointed fangs drawing from her pained mouth then. Never had I seen such a thing from my mother or father. I just couldn't take it anymore.

With a barely effortful strain of my arms, I broke from the restraints.

Giovanna choked out a squeak of surprise, and quickly rose from her chair, making the legs screech against the tile. We both remained silent for entirely too long.

"What the fuck," her words juddered out in a clipped groan of horror. "How in the hell did you do that?" she demanded, blanching a hundred shades whiter. The tremble in her lower lip could've been anger or wonder. Either way, I stood up, stunning myself.

How had I done that? Good sense warned me to hide my shocked relief. Whether or not Giovanna knew it, we were both experiencing a spontaneous moment of discovery. I had sat in that chair, braced against the restraints with all my might. For hours trying to break free without calling attention to myself. Nothing happened, the metal wouldn't give. Sergio had been right. Impenetrable, indestructible. But somehow. Somehow.

I lept and grabbed the pocket knife. Giovanna shifted to stop me but failed. Armed now, with something we knew wouldn't be lethal against her but just might cause enough damage, the temptation went out of her gaze.

"I don't want us to fight, Cam. We're a family."

I sucked in a breath through flared nostrils, kicked the chair over with a nudge.

"I'm leaving this fucking basement," there was no point in adding that she should not try to stop me, we both knew that she could not. I stuffed the knife into my joggers, the same from yesterday or however long it had been since we left this house for the airport.

Slowly holding her angelic round face in my sight, I skirted around her until the stairs waited but a yard away from me, never turning my back. She revolved her stance with my movement.

This woman. When I was seven she once lost sight of me in the Architecture and Design department at the massive Museum of Modern Arts in Manhattan. When the guard with the auburn beard brought us back together she nearly drowned me in a flood of her tears, squeezed me so tight I let out a dry sob and wished I had been a better son, one that wouldn't get lost in a museum and worry her so terribly. But when she released me, grasping both sides of my face, she wore the quivering, enthralled smile. Like the follower of a deity who'd witness their first miracle. "What would I do?" she said, wiping her eyes with the back of her hand, not caring about the waves of people turning to gape at us. "What would I do without you?"

"Where are you going?" She asked, setting her journal closed on her dining room chair.

I shook my head and turned away from her. Taking the stairs two at a time. Needing to see what was left. What could be salvaged from the world.

I went out of the front door, perplexed and drunk with exhaustion. The night air hit me like a cold slap across the face. Immediately I heaved, doubled over, stumbling off the porch and out into the open air. The night spun, or I spun on my heels. It was too easy. Moving my body was like taking flight in a zero-gravity chamber. I anchored myself, stooped over, with hands on my knees then peered up at the destruction before me.

The neighborhood lay in ruins, fires danced in the night sky, and the screams of dying neighbors peppered the air. Across the street, an old Cadillac rested on its side in the middle of Mr. and Mrs. Whittingham's yard. The passenger door had been torn off.

Giovanna followed me out, clamping on to the door frame, gliding elegantly down the steps in bare feet. She looked at me with pride.

"You're incredibly strong, Cam. Even taking the possible blood surge into account," she said softly. "It's like you didn't even feel the u.v... how the hell."

I ignored her ludicrous display of joy, and turned back to the chaos.

I would not speak the words in my mind, not yet. I was thinking two irreconcilable thoughts at once: how to find Markeya and how many of the people I had known my whole life would turn out to be one of them. I would find out on the way to rescue Markeya but the possibility of learning the truth nauseated me.

"I didn't expect any of this," Giovanna said, coming up to me, taking in the burning houses, the sounds of explosions and heavy duty vehicles crashing around us.

"Sergio certainly did." I said.

"But I'm just as caught off guard as you." Giovanna said.

I looked at her incredulously.

"I don't believe you. I don't believe anything you say anymore."

She turned a smug grin on me and opened her arms. "Your father did not utter a word to me about the Kine striking the human government. This war has been years in the making and I knew not a peep until today, I swear it," she said. "Or else I would have--- I would've warned you."

She pulled something from her cleavage. A smartphone. She handed it to me. It's body was warm. Fully charged, no service.

"What's this for?" I asked.

She sighed, "Well, if Markeya's still alive you'll need a little more than a knife to get through saving her. By the way, son. You can't simply stab one of them and end it that way. You'll have to destroy them, mutilate them."

Giovanna was beautiful in the evening, I didn't know if it was fear or hatred, but I thought about strangling her.

Instead, I left her side and staggered down the drive.

***

I found Markeya's friend's street and once there, snapped the neck of the man I found sitting cocksure on Nickie's porch swing, drinking from someone's family dog. My strength was incredible, but because of the state of things, I feared superhuman powers would do me little good.

They had taken over the whole neighborhood, and from the way Giovanna had spoken, I worried they'd taken over the whole world.

The night was dark, but the things ran past me. Ten-foot flames ate the insides of abandoned cars, some of them clearly crashed into light poles. Whole homes were set ablaze. But then I stumbled upon a sight that struck me with numb shock.

A mighty sequoia, probably a neighborhood green project. Someone might have planted it in honor of a nondescript historic figure. Blood pooled around its buried roots, and more dripped in a line down the enormous black trunk. I didn't want to, but I pulled out Giovanna's phone and swiped on the flashlight.

When I swept the glare up to the high branches and met the glassy dark-blue gaze of a dead man fitted in a tailored business suit. He was slumped over a thick arm of the tree, on his back, bent at a sickening angle and slashed ear to ear. It did not seem as if someone had posed the body this way, rather that he had landed in the tree after being thrown by some massive force.

My heart pounded in my chest as a driblet of blood from the crown of his head dropped on my cheek. I wiped it. A sweet coppery stench wafted from the smear across my fingers. I scrubbed it from my fingers and trundled down the street.

Making use of the old comforts I'd grown to expect, I took the sidewalk, knowing the smooth concrete would eventually lead me somewhere. I turned off the phone light when a shadow bursted from a patch of bushes out at me. A middle-aged man.

Naked as a baby. Skinny as a rake. Dick and balls swinging in the evening air.

I recoiled, but took care to conceal the alarm blitzing through my bloodstream. He stunk. He smiled.

The blood on his face flaked like neon rave paint. It covered his ghastly mouth and nose as he sauntered toward me. I flung the knife out and gasped it hammer style. "Take another step and I'll gut you."

Perhaps realizing, a little late, what I was, --- that I was like him--- the man pulled back and guffawed crazily.

"Why the long face?" He asked, arms stretching out, bird-like chest glistening. "Don't look like you've been having any fun, my friend."

I gritted my teeth against his stench, prepared to kill the man if I needed to. If I could. But by my next blink, he had flown past me.

"It's a free-for-all!" he screamed on his way down the street. "Dive in! Live a little! Live finally! Live forever!" The distance warped his voice maniacally. He hooked a curve around the four-way at top speed, hunting for another victim.

I ran too. It wasn't safe to walk. In the dark. In the open. I ran faster and harder than I'd ever run in the opposite direction. Hunting for Nickie's house, hunting for my culinary partner and our unborn child.

Soon enough I was standing on the McDaniels' porch, amidst a pile of the McDaniel's corpses. The mother lay prone across the father, the daughter Nickie prone across the mother.

I skidded to a stop at the porch steps and heaved dryly. The iron handrail in my grip slipped with something sticky and simultaneously slimy. Even in the dark I could tell the family had been dead a while. Their skin had gone slate, their limbs stiff.

Where was Markeya?

A grunt like some half-startled animal rumbled from the vicinity of gloom on the porch. I flinched, but pressed my lips together on the gasp that wanted to eek out of me.

I raised my eyes.

Behind the row of high hedges gloving the porch balusters, the curly head of the intruder shone under a dim sconced light. A sawing creak started from the wooden ceiling of the porch. Dreamily, the bench swing swayed back and forth from a set of iron hooks. The sound grated me. I stooped low and inched up the steps. Taking them slowly and timing my breaths. I felt an eternity pass before the figure came into relief. He might have been a country gentleman sleeping in the dewy night had he not been holding the straggly, mangled fur of the McDaniel's.

The thing saw me and sat bolt upright. He let out a hiss with fangs extended like a cobra in the desert.

I withdrew the knife, and the vampire leaped over the piles of bodies and threw itself against me. We tumbled down the stairs. An incredible jolt of fire shot up my body when the man chewed into my chest. I punched him once, with all my strength. He stopped. The night wind halted. The only sound was the sound of my breathing.

Amazingly, horrifically, my fist did not stop at the man's nose. Whether I had opened my eyes or the world around opened itself again to my senses, I could not tell. What I knew was the tableau suddenly flickered before my eyes after a brief delay. My arm was out stretched. The vampire's head hovered over me. But my fist had disappeared. Once the scene made sense, once I understood what I was seeing, I wanted my brain to melt.

The broken face of the vampire squeezed my balled fist. My hand was a part of his face then. I'd struck clean through him.

His heavy bulk stilled and as if it had wound up before a pitch, his steaming hot blood began to drizzle and deluge. It downpoured like a blistering, squalling rain in my eyes.

I tore my hand free of the shattered bone, pushing on his shoulder.

Admittedly frantic, I crawled back until I was yards away from the porch. The man's throat made little fluttering twitches. His broken face filled like a soup bowl with blood.

I was going to scream, I suddenly knew. For the first time in my life, I was going to scream shrill and stridently with all the lung capacity I had.

The blood, I thought. The human blood. I'd been forced fed and human blood and this had been the effect.

Struggling to rise from the damp grass beneath me, I was immediately met with a shocking force which sent me crashing back to the earth. The chill of the night seeped through my clothes contrasting the searing adrenaline drumming up my veins.

More had surged to the rescue of their friend. I rolled painfully to my side; eyes locked onto their forms. All colors and genders and in various states of undress. Their features illuminated by the cold porchlight. The odor of blood mixed with the scent of the dew-kissed grass beneath us, creating an unsettling concoction that raised the hair on my arms. I pulled myself along, army-crawling. Before I could find my hands and feet, I was overwhelmed and swarmed.

A male gripped my arm with a yanking twist. My bones bent unnaturally. My vision blurred with pain.

"Fuck you." I pulled back and struck him.

But that was all I managed before a woman, kneeled on top of me like a girlfriend. Her cold fingers grabbed my jaw. She leaned in close and assaulted me with a rough kiss. I threw her aside and bolted to my feet.

My heart was pounding then, not only because of the harrowing danger of being mobbed, but the truly astounding spectacle of my own strength.

The woman flew at me again, screaming. I palmed her face and she bit down. The ligaments from the third knuckle snapped. I slung her to the ground. And spotted the knife. Nearly thrown under the porch steps, and as soon as I was able to grab it, something landed on my back.

I twisted and jammed the knife into the vampire's throat and yanked the man's head back, bringing the blade clean out of the front.

You have to destroy them.

Swept up in some kind of mad mental torrent, I began swiping the knife and hitting every target, but they kept rising up again. Stabbing alone did no good. I could've stabbed and stabbed all night and gotten no closer to entering that house. No closer to Markeya.

You have to mutilate them.

You had to break them. You have to pull them apart. You have to take things from them they could not go without until they stopped. Until they stopped coming. I did for hours it seemed like.

Until I was crawling up the stairs, injured, exhausted, and dripping in rhubarb red. Thankfully, I felt nothing, though every inch of me sloshed with still wet blood. I had killed. Since the airport when they first attacked I hadn't been sure if I'd ever killed anyone but laying next to the McDaniels' bodies, I remembered. Clarity. Full flourishing clarity perhaps brought on by the familiar heat of their blood came twirling back to me. I had shot and shot them in the airport, and they had kept coming. Then I began to break them into pieces, tear them apart. The body parts on the carpet. Had I done that?

I dragged myself to standing. My own blood mixed noxiously with the blood of strangers.

I walked through the McDaniels' front door.

***

In the grand foyer, I found her, still alive but barely, her golden skin leeched pale. Blood like a halo around her head. We prepared banana pancakes for our first assignment. Markeya flipped the first and it flopped out of the skillet and onto the stove top, wet batter splashed up her apron. I wanted to laugh, but fought the urge, but a snort betrayed me. That was the first time Markeya's bright, gold-streaked eyes swooped in my direction. She halted me that moment in the classroom test kitchen.

My shoes squeaked on the foyer floor. The lights from a mini chandelier shafted down with scorching power. Her eyes shifted to me again. Dull and narrow until, I supposed, she recognized me. The light resurged angry and adoring.

I took an excruciatingly slow step forward, like a man walking in a dream. I tried to tunnel my vision and see less of the scene, see only Markeya. But my attention took in things it hungered to keep. Horrible things. The piece of rope tied to her wrist, broken or chewed through. I knelt beside her. I wanted to lay next to her, pull her into my arms but for the first time since we met I feared touching the love of my life. What if a touch collapsed the thread tethering her to the world.

"Baby," my lips moved but I didn't hear my own words. I gently patted back her hair away from her brow. "Baby, I'm sorry." This wasn't the plan. The way things were supposed to happen in my head looked much different than this.

Pictured coaxing the McDaniels' rich people by every standard, out of their sophisticated safe room. They'd be rationing out food and water, running a generator to keep up with plumping and air circulation. They'd be waiting out rescue from the U.S army when I arrived. Was that naïve? I had expected to find humvees thundering down every street, Camos directing the populace to safe zones. But none of that had happened.

Outside of the vampires tearing down the world, the neighborhood was a ghost town. And that was because the vampires started with the armies, the government, the leadership of humanity. The rash of killings that had struck down mayors, senators, governors, top ranking military personnel. None of it was the doing of a serial killer with high-clearance. Not a strategized attack of a foreign enemy. It was them. It was slow death.

Markeya sighed, or was it a whimper. Newer coagulating pools of blood, breached and rifted through the darker layers near her neck had been.

The source of the blood made itself unmistakably known. A jagged bite on her delicate shoulder glared red and vicious. I spotted several more bites next to the largest wound, some criss-crossing each other. She'd been drunk from, kept alive and drank from more.

Tears stung my eyes. "What do I do?" I whispered, "Baby." There was no one to fight, no one to shoot.

Those wide expressive eyes melted me. Glazed, pain filled eyes. Their lids lowered. "No." I took her limp hand.

"Please. Please don't," I whispered. Every nerve in my body screamed for action, for a way to save her. I felt a quiver in my trembling hands, my fingers tracing the cold, lifeless skin of her cheek. The powdery scent of dead house plants, earth and metallic rain hung heavily in the air, I bit into my wrist until blood trickled, prepared to feed her, desperate to save her life.

The clamp of my teeth into my own wrist was as sudden to me as a thunderclap. I felt no pain as my new longer fangs sank through my flesh. The act was driven by instinct, by adrenaline. In defiance of all reason or rational thought.

It was as if the very essence of my being had been reduced to this singular purpose, to bridge the gap between life and death with a drop of my own life's blood.

Markeya's eyes shut again, and I began to suck on the bite like a vacuum pump, pulling my streaming blood to a stronger rush. Pain and warmth radiated from the wound, mingling with the sweat on my skin. In the dim light, droplets of crimson welled up then ran down my arm. Ready to offer her salvation. I sighed. I nearly sobbed. Rushing to adjust her head so I could press my gush wrist to her still lips.

Jostled, Markeya opened her eyes and turned her head weakly away.

"Stop. Don't," she pleaded softly, "Don't make me what you are. Let me go, Cam."

I shook my head slowly back and forth. My blood pumping out of me like a jet, I cradled her head, and slid my hand down the length of her body until I reached her midriff. Such a well of protest wanted to climb out of me. What about our baby, what about our lives? How will I live without you?

Instead of any of this, I let go of a sob.

"I don't want to let you go baby. I can't." But how could I bring myself to do it? Change my little bossy chef into one of those things?

Markeya's eyes filled with a mixture of fear and understanding. "Cam, Don't. I'll be worse than dead," she said, her voice trembling.

"Markeya," I whispered, my own voice choking me. "I love you."

She didn't respond. Her eyes shut. I squeezed her hand, but this time the gesture produced nothing. "Markeya, did you hear me?" I muttered, "I said I love you."

I felt her final inhale, against my body. Markeya breathed her last breath in my arms, leaving me for good. Leaving me alone. I pulled her to my chest, embracing her yielding body against me. No matter how deeply I inhaled, I couldn't get my voice to expel. Until all at once, my body let go of a full-bodied wail.

***

I stumbled from the porch and ambled to the back yard; the sky bore down on my shoulders like it wanted to smash me to pieces. Black unfathomable, not a star twinkling. I wished it would fall and snuff me out. Nicky's family had a tool shed tucked into a shadowy corner beside their back yard fence. A giant charcoal grill perched next to it. There would be no more backyard barbecues or birthday pool parties. Not for anyone.

I found a shovel in the shed, brand new from its appearance. Looked like I would be the first to use it. The irony of that struck me with hard, swarming gooseflesh. I dug four holes, as deeply as I could. I dug until the sky began to swirl the first gray stripes of a sweltering dawn.

Then I carried Nicky and her parents one by one and laid them in the Earth, covering their bodies, their serene faces with the loose soil until no one could see them. I carried Markeya, in my arms, my nose pressed against her hair and carefully laid her body in the makeshift grave. A rest in place. My tears fell, warm and plenty, in the dirt with her, as I laid shovels and shovels of dirt over her, until the pale purple pajamas disappeared until she disappeared. Then I laid in the dewy grass beside her and stared up as the white beach ball grew higher and higher and peaked through the branches of the neighbor's pecan tree.

I drove Mr. Henry's truck to Ortega Forest where Ryan spent weekends with his father. The neighborhood was known as one of the wealthiest in Jacksonville. One of the wealthiest and one of the safest. But I was sure that was no longer true.

The sun poured through the windshield in hot stabbing rays. I didn't remember if I'd ever felt sunlight bite down the layers of my skin so deeply. Was this my frayed imagination? My mind pulling apart at the seam? Or was the sun setting an itch to my skin like the first flare of an allergic reaction? I found myself eyeing my white-knuckled grip on the steering wheel and watching those knuckles turn beet red.

I lowered the visor, but it helped not at all, so I rolled down the windows, and pumped up the A.C letting some of the heat escape. I regretted the decision almost immediately when a foul moist gust entered the cab with me. This was not the ordinary Floridian humidity. This was an assailing almost intentional dankness. It seemed like the air was wetter than it had ever been. Wetter than the aftermath of the hardest downpour. Like the Earth contained more ocean than it had the night before. And the wetness had a smell, an eye-burning stink. I rolled the window back up and felt my stomach twitch with an indescribable hunger.

It was in the air now. The hunger. I couldn't escape the smell of blood no matter what I tried; the thirst was a part of me.

We've always been, as Giovanna promised.

Finally, I arrived at Ryan's two-story country style brick house. I've been here many times throughout my middle school and high school years. Mr. Obeshaw was always welcoming and kind, insanely smart and even interesting though he worked as a chief actuary at an insurance company. Which meant he really loved data analysis and risk assessment. But he was a pretty good dart thrower and let us drink beers when we stayed in for the weekend. Ryan was his only son, and he adored him. The two had an enormous number of secret handshakes and inside jokes. I loved hanging around them, and watching the father and son relationship I could only dream of having. It took all the fight I had to get out of the car and step out onto the Obeshaws' shellac driveway.

The rest of the neighborhood, besides that dewy dankness, was as dead as anything ever could be. When usually you could find the neighbors sitting in their yard or walking their dogs on the sidewalks, I hadn't even seen a car pass down the beautifully paved road the whole way through the winding blocks.

They're all dead, I thought. Looking up at Ryan's house, the blue façade and the dark upstairs windows glaring at me like dreary, murderous eyes, I realized Ryan was dead too.

He and his father. They had to be. The onslaught had been so penetrating, so merciless there couldn't have been a survivor behind the meager walls of a brick house. They would've needed a fortress, an underground bunker to survive. But I paced up the drive anyway then ascended the porch steps. After what happened to Markeya, my Markeya I had to at least chance saving my best friend.

I pulled the knife from my pocket and opened it. Blood glazed the blade.

With no surprise, glass sparkled in shattered pieces all over the porch. The glass sidelites had been kicked out, and the cold air inside Ryan's house wafted against my body. I pushed the already unlatched door open and stepped inside.

"Ryan?" I called. There was no answer, "anybody here?"

I stepped into a foyer with high ceilings and marble floors. The walls were adorned with elegant artwork, and a crystal mini chandelier hung above, casting a warm glow.

A grand staircase to the left led to the upper floor, while double doors on the right opened into a well-appointed living room. The living room hung in darkness and a grand fireplace looked cold with just the large windows allowing natural light to filter in.

Moving deeper into the house, I noticed signs of chaos – overturned furniture, askew paintings, and broken glass on the once-pristine floors.

I scanned the upstairs staircase. A heavy wooden dresser had slid halfway down the stairs as if someone with enormous strength had launched it from one of the bedrooms.

"Ryan, it's Cam. Are you here or not?"

An answering groan from behind me and to the right.

Behind a tall wall sectioning off the entrance and living room from the wide kitchen, a faint light glowed. I approached holding the knife up, peeking around the wall.

What I saw in that kitchen made me instantly falter back and flush myself against the dividing wall.

I held my breath. Fuck. Then came another groan from the thing in the Obeshaw house.

That was Ryan, raiding his own refrigerator, like we had countless times after wrestling practice but also that wasn't Ryan. Not at all.

I looked again. This time taking in the full scope of the scene. Food spread across the floor, vegetables, fruits, and spilled milk splashed on the counters. It looked like a scene out of an 80's movie one featuring little havoc-wreaking monsters searching for a late-night snack. Except those movies were pretty tame on the visuals, whereas the Obeshaws' kitchen also looked like a scene from a slasher film.

Bloody handprints, shoe prints, and castoff in great strokes up the walls, and the backsplash. Looked like someone had taken a paintbrush and tried to cover every square inch of white space they could reach with bright red.

The groaning belonged to nothing human or animal. It was the sound of something else entirely, something that shouldn't have existed, something that shouldn't have a voice. It was pain, it was suffering. It was deeper than normal vocal cords could manage, and the groans lasted longer than human lungs could hold breath.

I bit down on my lip and felt my heart squeezing in my throat. Please don't let that really be Ryan, I begged, I prayed. Just dammit, not him, anyone but him.

I took one final look, leaning my head to the side slowly, and stopped.

He was looking right back at me. Straight into my eyes.

His brown face slick and glossy with blood. His smile was a pattern of red dripping teeth. His eyes were wet and vein-struck.

"Cam, bro," the thing with Ryan's face said. He came toward me in a way that was somehow hulking at Ryan's lean size. "One of those things from the news bit me at the community center. Can you believe it?"

I faltered back.

"Ah, come on man, it's not that bad is it?" he said, looking genuinely hurt. He glanced back at the steel fridge door, where a worn reflection peered back at him. "Ok it's pretty bad," he muttered. "But I know it'll get better. All I need is something to drink. Is that why you came? You can read my mind can't you man? It's like we share a soul isn't it? Like we're real blood brothers."

He was walking toward me, but I matched him with a backwards step for every step he took. "Ryan, man, you're not doing too well."

"I know."

He circled me, but I revolved with him, unwilling to risk my back turned to him. Now he was backing me up toward the kitchen.

"You know what's funny," he said, or I think he said it. It sounded as if something inside him was speaking for him, something he'd swallowed which was trying to come up again. His throat kept making these nauseating clicking noises, like lodged hiccups. "I detected this incredible smell in the air. Just a few minutes ago. I caught a whiff of it. Remarkable, like a gourmet dessert, that ice cream sundae they sell at serendipity. And I thought where do I get some of that, and then you walked in, Cam. A coincidence?"

"Alright, that's enough, Ryan. Stay the fuck back."

"Why?" he said, imitating wounded innocence. "You're my best friend, Cam."

He was right, I'd come to save him, come to take him away from this apocalypse with me but I'd been too late.

Ryan raised his arms out toward me and at the end of his wrist joints his hands were like claws. "Please help me, Camelot. I'm so thirsty."

He lept, I dodged him and he fell against the counter, knocking over appliances, a glass mixing bowl fell and shattered on the floor.

I moved back a few paces more until I was nearly in the dining room, and that's when I tripped over something large and soft. I caught myself on another partition wall just as I would've landed backward into Mr. Obeshaw's open stomach.

I gagged. Stumbled away and looked at Ryan through a blur of horror. He looked too at his father's eviscerated form on the floor. Like a child who'd been caught red handed stealing from the candy jar, Ryan sighed at me. "That wasn't my fault," he whined, "I told him I was thirsty and he tried to tie me up in the basement. Some good parent, huh? I didn't want to have to do that."

"Fuck, Ryan." I shot. The shaking in my voice terrified me. "Damn it, what have you done?"

He raised both hands as if in resignation, then huffed. The asshole actually huffed. "Just try this once to be a little empathetic, yeah? I'm in pain, Cam, it hurts like hell, like nothing you'll ever know, ok? Stop judging everyone on grit. We can't all be Mr. hardass."

"God dammit, Ryan stay the fuck back!"

"Selfish prick.!" He rushed into the dining room and in one great heave knocked over the antique table his dad won in the divorce settlement. In a split second, he lept and cleared the table remains and practically landed in my arms.

Ryan had tackled me in the past, during backyard football games on thanksgiving break, but this time he was like a torpedo, with teeth. Suddenly we were reeling back, blasting through the glass sliding door in a hail of shards.

The impact against the patio brick sent lightning off in my head. But I had no time to spin. Immediately, Ryan clamped down on my arm. Fang knife sharp and precise. I swung the knife again and again, plunging the blade into his ribs, but nothing stopped him. I threw him off, and he went easier than I'd expected, launching back feet overhead, he crashed into the glass door like a frisbee. I snapped up to my feet hungry, thirsty and angry.

I pinned Ryan to the ground, crushing his throat with my forearm like a baton. Bloody fangs seething, he bit at me, cloudy tears welled then spilled from his eyes. I could believe what I was seeing, one of the only people on this Earth who knew about my childhood fear of snakes. The boy who dared me to eat a cricket and filmed it on my first fishing trip. First Markeya and then my best friend. "Please man," I begged him over the sounds of that nonhuman groaning. "I love you man."

Ryan's eyes glistened like a rabid dog, but he stilled for barely a second, and as he did the sun part a stack of clouds, the blade of sunlight cut the patio in half horizontally. The length of the light bisected Ryan at the collar, and the hot smell of singed skin rose off of him. He looked at me as if he could see into my mind. A gentle smile played at his lips, and he coughed as a spread of hive-like welts blistered over his face. The sun baked away his skin.

"I wish," he croaked, "I wish I'd been right in the parking lot. I wish that had been the last time you saw me." And he started to laugh, gut-deep guffawing filled with plaintive resignation. "Thanks man," he said, the sun ringing down on us, his hairline cracked along the edges, shriveling up. "You're doing me a solid." He laughed again. His hand touched my arm. I bit down on my lip, as slowly, Ryan quieted, and the color went out of his rich dark skin. His hand fell from my arm. His pupils expanded, he lay still.

"Ryan?" I called, searching his face.

No response. I moved.

When I did so, the blanching of his skin intensified at a speed beyond anything natural. Ryan turned gray.

Seeing this, my heart thundered like galloping horse hooves in my chest, and I broke all over with hive-like goosebumps and a clammy cold sweat. I realized then that I was going to throw up. I was going to puke in my lap and spend all day trying not to die because of the smell.

I got up and staggered as far away from Ryan's body as I could and hurled in a patch of Bahia grass.

All I could hear was the screaming in my mind. The awful shriek of hopelessness.

I stumbled from one dark corner of the city to the next, driven solely by the need for sustenance. I refused to think about anything else. A sturdy brick wall erected around the atrocities I had seen, around Markeya, around Ryan, around our dead neighbors. Those innocent people whose lives had been trimmed off like the ends of string beans. So uselessly brutal. My cheeks had turned raw from scowling, fighting true tears. But I couldn't let myself fall to shards and splinters as clearly natural selection and survival of the fittest had made a U-turn for human society. If I was going to be picked down to my bones or turned to petrified woods like Ryan, I wanted it to happen because I'd had my revenge, and I was good and damn ready. My focus was unwavering – revenge first, everything else second. Until then, all my focus fixed on finding my next meal.

One night, I came upon a group of vampires in black combat uniforms, dragging people out of hiding and loading them in rusted beater vans. I watched as they shot mercilessly at those who tried to escape. I knew I should do something to help, but instead, I found myself paralyzed with misery and heartache, unable even to try.

I'd been sleeping in the truck for days, parked wherever I thought no one would bother me, ---in the center of the landing, on the transformer bridge, almost always with the windows rolled up trying to escape that humid stink.

That funk, it was like a cloud, floating above the city wherever I went. It seemed my hometown, my city was dying, decaying and I was living in its rotting corpse. Downtown Jacksonville, the 2.2 square mile urban core of Jacksonville lay in eerie disarray as the vampire population had taken control of the city's heart.

Its landmarks bore the scars of chaos, making it almost unrecognizable. I didn't even bother to look out of my windows as I careered around the blocks.

Wells Fargo Center and Bank of America Tower, which had once been symbols of prosperity, now stood as foreboding monoliths, their windows shattered, and banners tattered. The neon lights that once adorned the Florida Theatre flickered intermittently, casting an unsettling glow on the deserted streets.

The vibrant St. Johns River, which usually teemed with activity, now mirrored the bleakness of the city, of the calamity. The Main Street Bridge stood open. It was usually overrun with traffic but was now replaced by silence. Abandoned water taxis bobbed idly below it, while the docks, once the launching point for riverside events, were left in neglect.

I drove Mr. Henry's truck where I had been driving every night. Finding the small groups of vampires who were sniffing out human survivors. The pocketknife, I realized, didn't work on Ryan and it wouldn't work on any of them. I had to use creativity and the violent power of thirst to overpower two, and sometimes three, vampires at once. Their blood, it pained me to say, was sweeter and sweeter every time.

The night in question, however, I traversed Bay street and Ocean to find the riverside plaza, formerly known as the landing buzzing with activity. I parked in the glow of hundreds of streetlights. It was as if someone had turned back time for just this area, and Saturday night in downtown Jacksonville was back and roaring. The engine of sports cars growled, bar patrons perused, and bands performed into several venues.

I felt out of place in jeans and a dirty blood-streaked tee shirt. Everyone else sported leather, expensive shoes. Some women walked around wearing jean shorts and those colorful little patches that cover their nipples and nothing more. It was surreal, even with the broken glass and blood marring the streets, downtown looked the same. A little raunchier, a little sexier but the same. Almost as if the gouging of the city hadn't bothered these people at all. As if vampires thrived in the evident destruction.

And then I realized making my way down Ocean St, head down, hands in pockets, what made the scene much more sinister. The men dressed in all black, standing at odd street corners holding auto snipers. I'd already spotted five of them. Two at the private art gallery and three passing the Florida Theatre mom once dragged me to for a viewing of Hamilton.

I shuddered to think what could be housed in those magazines. What could the bullets be made of that would keep the peace so effectively. I stalked down the street, not bothering to acknowledge those who knocked into me, curling their upper lips and snarling subtly.

Up ahead the outside flooded with rainbow exterior lights the streets were overrun with vampires. It was like a festival, the concert stage had been set up, and the amplifiers were shredding the usual quiet. There was loud chanting, though I could make out the words, the music was too loud.

The skate park whirled with skaters performing aerial tricks. The rumble and squeaking of their wheels on the concrete ramps hurt my ears.

Abandoned restaurants and bars along Ocean Street displayed shattered glass windows, and nothing else. It felt lonely, ghostly coming to the end of the street. That was until the live music pumping out of The Shim Sham Room was interspersed with shouting and shrieks of pain. Coming for the alley around the corner of the lounge. I approached quietly.

Deep in the throats of these darkened places, the city's survivors, those who hadn't fallen to the vampire onslaught, sought refuge in the shadows, in underground tunnels, under bridges, in whatever cracks they could squeeze into.

I was not seeking to hunt them. I couldn't fathom the taste of human blood on my tongue. I could handle the thought that I was the monster we all feared hid under our beds as children. Not when I was still unsure what I was, and what I was becoming. I was, however, seeking the hunters of the hunted.

Desperate for blood and energy. That I couldn't deny. The need had finally won its victory over my defiance. Crouched now, the closer I paced to the screams, the tighter the cramps clenched in my belly, pain against pain, like metal against metal.

The night was not black but navy blue and inordinately hot. I squinted my eyes in the darkness. Three shadowy figures flitted around, slumped forms laying at their feet. A dumpster creaked as a body was hurled against it. An anguished cry and an answering cackle resounded in the night.

Two figures cowered on the dirty alley floor amidst broken glass and garbage. I heard their voices pleading, crying. The three assailants, standing like erect statues stood over them under the gleam of sheer moon light, hemming their victims. The groaning voices, deep like Ryan's had been, utter some otherworldly gestures to one another, laughter rang out again. Then the vampires fell upon their humans and drained them until nothing remained - not even a single drop of blood left behind. The last scream died with a crack.

Their meal taken, the group turned on their way. I slinked into the alley behind them, senses heightened, anticipation for my nightly relief growing into a steady thump against my temples. The stink of the air and the garbage seemed to cling to my every step as I trailed them.

Halfway toward the exit of the alley, one of them stopped. Froze in place as if he'd felt a cold breath touch his neck, and as he stopped the other two halted. They turned in unison to face me. I lunged at the closest male vampire, determined to take the fight to them.

The impending clash was like a collision of worlds, a struggle that would determine the course of this fateful night and I loved every second of it. The very essence of survival, both theirs and mine had become the only sensible thing about life anymore.

When morning broke and reality hit me once again, my guilt was unbearable. I'd become what I hated most - a monster that preys on innocent victims in order to survive. But worse than that: I'd betrayed Markeya's memory by refusing to save those people from certain death. Tears filled my eyes as I realized the magnitude of what I'd done. If Markeya were still alive, she would have stopped me from committing such an act.

I drove for what seemed like forever, or at least until the gas ran out of Mr. Henry's truck. I thought about checking the long bed for a hand fuel pump, but no way was any gas station operable. I abandoned the idea and explored on foot. Traveling until I found a coastline I walked in the sand on the beach. I swam in the ocean until the salt water itched my skin.

I broke into an abandoned sandwich shop near a shopping center and made myself a roast beef Swiss, then promptly vomited in the back.

***

St. Augustine, Florida

There was a historic fortress near a majestic river in the center of town. The structure looked like a medieval castle with cannons and plaques retelling the history of Spanish occupancy of Florida. The Castillo de San Marco.

The monument occupied a huge grassy lot, groups and couples lounged on picnic blankets, some of them naked, like the world had not just ended. The interior of the castle, paved with rough coquina rock, had been structured like a 16th century soldiers' quarters. The space impersonated a set up for the National Geographic documentaries I used to be obsessed with. I always marveled at the architectural feats of ancient civilizations, the construction of places built so strong and innate they withstood era after era.

I sank deeper into the building, into another room, where a kitchen had been built with fake flames flickering in a clay oven. Plastic bread loafs, fruit, sweetmeats and pastries had been stacked on dilapidated shelves.

I stuck my hand into the oven and touched the uneven, rocky surface.

"It's not real you know," a voice from behind me said, "There's no need to cook anymore. You only eat what you hunt now."

"Stay back." I said to the woman with the half-pinned curls. A pair of sharp cat-eye frames which made her eyes large and ethereal. She peered from the entry door, where an exit sign glowed overhead. The dark shadows of the cave-like gallery hid most of her form and created curves and dips.

"You look famished." She pulled out a vial of blood from her pocket "Looking for this?

"What is that?"

I saw her smile but also heard it. In some ways, the noises of the world, what sound was by nature had changed. I heard colors, animals from miles away.

"An apple pie." Her lips were painted a bellicose lime green.

Strapped to her chest was some tight cutout, patchwork top with thick white stitching and a stand collar.

"Did you just leave a rave?" I asked.

"No, I left an abandoned boutique."

She peered down at her ensemble, playfully flicked up the heel of one of her boots. The material was so covered in buckles I easily surmised she had to zip them in the back to put them on.

The vial she held glinted in the faux firelight, bright red.

"Catch," she tossed it to me. I caught it.

"My name's Payton, what's yours?"

I said nothing, and instead opened the vile to take a sniff of the viscous liquid inside. Human blood.

"Never tried it?" she asked.

Oh, I'd had tried it. I'd been forced to try it. And that excruciating day marked the last time I felt like anything beyond walking bones and nerves. Without it, vampire and animal blood was a piss-poor substitute, which was why I'd avoided the indulgence of human blood thus far. Anything that delicious and powerful means to control.

Suddenly Payton stood before me, too close, a veil of perfumed breath touched my face. She plucked the vial from fingers. "Head back, say ah."

I peered at her. A head shorter than me but somehow exuding a strange power which splintered my automatic objection.

Was I still in shock about Markeya, my friends, family, the military? Yes, a haven of shock but the shock was wearing off.

"Drink it." Payton said patiently.

I did so. The blood touched my lips and ignited me from within.

"It's not much but it's home, our home and now yours," Payton said from the driver seat of a stolen Fiat. I knew it was stolen because she bragged about still having the hand of the vampire who'd stolen it from a suburban family just when everything... went to shit.

By my calculation approximately five weeks had passed since I escaped the Paratus estate and watched the love of my life and my best friend die. That was over a month, but the anguish of it was like a fresh 3rd degree burn.

The driveway we pulled into was a good five miles from the Castillo, and for a place across the street from the beach, the two-story house was magnificent. Not overly large but for the location, prime real estate. The winding stone path swelled up a hill, curving to the entrance of a huge porch.

***

At a huge property overlooking the wild, shattering Atlantic, we exited the mint green Fiat, Payton's car. I spotted a lawn sign announcing the third day of a writers' conference. A cascade of chills ran over my skin, head to toe. We've all been caught with our pants down I thought.

"Hey, you coming inside?" Payton asked, she had walked well ahead of me, mounting the steps with a mischievous slanted grin on lime green painted lips. I like the colors in her hair, the wet look of her leather pants. It was distracting and absurd, in a way that was somehow soothing.

"Do you have another vial?" I asked.

She scoffed, "You fledglings are insatiable."

I followed. "How long have you been... one of them?"

"One of you?" she said with a laugh, "A vampire? About ten years ago I dated this tattoo artist, he was weird, like you, green eyes too. I cheated on him and he gave me the gift of immortality as revenge. Haven't seen him since."

We went inside the house.

The writer's conference had been interrupted but it hadn't ended. Those who'd been in attendance still were. Except they were no longer discussing their latest work in progress with a side of gourmet biscotti. They were tied up like the participants in a sex game. Scarves and neck ties and pantie holes. I guess no one could find any rope. None of the humans tied to the furniture looked afraid, I suppose days had passed since the last time they'd been anxious for a release that wasn't coming.

I peered at them as I entered, the room was large enough to see them all at once though they were spread out to different corners. Some were near the fireplace, others tied to the coffee table.

There was a man shivering on the floor, wearing nothing but his jeans and socks. Someone had tied a bundle of fake roses together stem to stem and had placed them on his head like a crown.

I waited for incredulous horror to overtake me but all I felt was thirsty.

"You swore, Paypay, no more strays."

A voice rang out from the open kitchen. A man as tall as me but with a better sense of style and a generally more pleasant expression rounded the corner. He locked eyes with me and smiled.

"Scratch that, this one can stay." He drank what looked like a bloody Mary, a celery stick poked out the crystal highball glass. He winked at me. I would've bet my life there was more than vodka and tomato juice floating around in there.

"Nice, beard. I'm A.J." he said, offering a hand for me to shake, I did. He was stronger than he looked. I rubbed the wiry fluff on my chin.

"Camden," I said.

He smirked, "I like it. Like the city in New Jersey? Are you turned or pureblood Camden?"

I shrugged.

A.J gave a smug smirk, "Memory problems or what?"

"He's pureblood but new to the hunt," Payton said with a relish."

"I was turned two years ago," A.J offered. "Bitten by an ex friend who I disinvited from my graduation party. I was supposed to be a doctor, Camden. I'd settled on hematology funny enough." He took a deep sip of his drink. His lips and teeth came away deeply red. "So he bites me while I was on my way to pull my car into the garage. I think he meant for me to die, but I found him at our mutual friend's house and bit his ass back. Ugly what jealousy does to beautiful people. But I'm learning to love it." A.J smiled wide, gulped his drink and winced. "Well except for this whole kerfuffle going on with the 'army of the Kine.'"

Payton grunted, rolling her eyes. "Don't even get me started. This sucks"

She walked past me, entering the kitchen to open the fridge. "Come here," she called.

"Who are you guys talking to?" Another woman and man peek into the kitchen. I turned to look at them and saw them both start.

"Camden." A.J crooned. "This is Heather and Grayson. Heather is a pure blood." He drew the words out slowly as if to impress upon how impressed I should be. And Grayson is her on again-off again beefcake."

Heather was a dark woman, the color of a sparrow, eyes like a tabby cat, bright vivid irises. She finger-waved at me.

The man, Grayson, black hair black eyes said nothing. He busied himself directing a human woman dressed in only a bathrobe, to sit at the little breakfast nook adjoining the kitchen.

Without his prompting the woman rolled up the sleeves of her robe. Her elbows revealed teeth marks, indentations and streaks of blood on both arms. Instead of running to the sink and hurling, I felt my blood steer with a tumultuous want, a thirst almost sexual in nature.

As if just settling on something, A.J pointed at me with his dislodged celery stick. "When was the last time you had a Sub Q by the way."

"What the hell is that?" I asked.

Heather and Payton glanced at me in shock . "Ultraviolet protection," Payton said slowly as if speaking to an incredibly dense individual. "Heather, go grab the kit from upstairs. I'll get started on the drinks.

"Don't spill it like last time." A.J grimaced at Grayson.

Human blood. I could smell it from where I stood. Payton suddenly pulled out a blender attachment from the fridge filled to the brim with Bloody Mary.

***

I did ecstasy once. I was fourteen and pretty sure I could handle anything. Luckily, I was right. In addition, I had no idea at the time that I would want to join the wrestling team anytime soon, so there was no harm there.

I would be the one of my friend group to answer the question, once and for all.

What's it feel like to be high out of your mind? I bought one pill for fifty dollars from a kid who lived in the neighborhood directly behind Avondale Prep. He only ever emerged from his house to watch the cheerleaders practice and to peddle what goop he'd stolen from his uncle, whom he claimed belonged to a motorcycle gang.

Greg Weatherford dared me to take one of the little white tablets and, as all teenage boys knew, to not answer the dare was a capital offense.

I woke up the next morning on Ryan's trampoline, with my brain intact. I remembered everything, so the memory loss thing was debunked, however I was not sure which of those memories really happened and which were an exaggeration. My friends helped me sort through the bulk of it. Most of their tales I believed. The rest, I thought they may have made up.

A ten-day stint drunk on blood and sex was like that high. Almost exactly, but instead drowning in the paranoia of discovery and overdose, I spent days and nights grasping the concept of immortality.

What was immortality?

"You need to wash your hair." Payton rolled away from me. "Everything, you smell.!

Of course, I smelled. I'd been covered in blood for 4 days straight. I was a splatterpunk feign.

"Take a shower." She got out of bed, topless and pulled her hair into a sloppy bun. "I'm going downtown today and see what I can find you in the way of clothes. I stared at her back, the slopes of her delicate muscles along her shoulders, so taut, so smooth, so dangerous. Who was this woman?

"You don't mind off the rack Gucci do you?" she laughed. "Last time I visited the town center, looters had stripped all of Nordstrom to the fiberglass."

She left without a word more, and I uprooted myself from the bed we shared and slugged to the bathroom.

The last time I'd spent so much time at a beach house had been during a family vacation to Saint. Barts. That trip had been so refined and upscale that I'd felt foolishly pampered. The resort was immaculate to the point of being nearly sterile. A speck of dust on a room service tray would've made the grounds manager faint. There hadn't been any sand mixed in blood turning a dull brown on my feet, no steadily growing beard turning wiry and reddish overtaking my face.

I'd never been so dirty inside, never so hopeful to distract myself from that filth through the dishevelment of my appearance. The blood and sand did not wash off easily after all. Filth and debauchery had been my only smoke screen for a while and it didn't want to go.

I shaved the clumps from my chin and patted my face dry. In the mirror, I saw a guy resembling my old self looking back. But after three months, I had no idea who that old self was anymore. And the new guy didn't want to get to know him anyway.

The bathroom door swung open as I wiped shaving cream from my face.

"Payton, don't come bothering me, I did what you asked."

"Not Payton." A small voice breathed.

I looked up and saw Heather. High peach color, blonde straight hair. I smiled. "Hi."-

Heather's presence took me by surprise, and my initial confusion quickly turned into unrestrained lust. She was a welcome change from the chaos and uncertainty that had become my life over the past few months.

"Hey there," she greeted me.

"Is Payton back yet?" I asked, still holding onto my razor, streaked with shaving cream.

"Nope, she probably won't come back until sunrise, you know how she is." Heather stepped closer, her gaze roaming over my face as if she were assessing the newly revealed features beneath the lather. "You look nice again. Not that you didn't before. Sometimes though I worry about you. Nice transformation," she said, her voice dropping to a sultry tone. "You're handsome when you're clean, Camden."

A warmth spread through me, and I actually laughed, not out of horror this time but pure amusement. I slid an arm around her waist and pulled her close. "Well, I couldn't stay in that gruesome state forever," I replied, my grin growing wider. "You were starting to look scared every time I looked at you."

Heather pressed herself closer to me, her feline gaze locking onto mine. "Fresh starts can be exciting," she purred, her fingers lightly grazing my chest. "And I can think of some ways to make this one unforgettable."

I couldn't deny the attraction that had always simmered between us, but it was difficult to sneak around Payton who seemed to have a six sense for every thought in my head and every meaning behind my facial expressions.

I had never cheated on anyone before, I'd never even cheated on a test. I didn't know what I was anymore. An addict, a scoundrel, a killer. All I knew was I wanted Heather while I held her in my arms.

"Heather," I began, my voice soft but earnest, "I've missed you. These past few months have been... something else. Terrible I guess." But the blood made it bearable.

Every week one of my housemates, especially Grayson and Payton, left and found more. And I kept the house running for them, and protected the grounds like a highly paid security guard. I replaced the storm windows, and resealed the deck, trimmed the trees hanging over the area fence in the backyard. At night I took the longest shift to stand guard, most of the time relieving A.J only two hours into his shift.

My contribution finally convinced the group to cut down on human captives. They were keeping 4 at a time. We were down to one willing participant who slept in a bed instead of tied to a table leg in the living room. As long as no one decided to act like a selfish prick, the man would sleep as many nights as he could stand amongst vampires.

 Keeping the house safe and liveable distracted from the thirst, but left me tacky and languid later.

Heather moved even closer, her lips hovering just inches from mine. "I've missed you too, Camden," she confessed, her breath warm against my skin. "I was starting to grow depressed after weeks without you inside me."

I swallowed. "I'm sorry."

As her lips finally met mine, I thought that maybe, just maybe, this time the indulgence would open my eyes to new avenues. Maybe I'd grow sincerely comfortable with the evils in the world and all I had done to go on living in it. The question of why I settled on persisting in through the nightmares and flashbacks. Possibly because I felt none of it. None of the loss. None of the grief. None of the betrayal. I'd forgotten why I had wished for death months before. Or rather I'd learned to

I undressed her quickly, a quick tug on the zipper at her nape and the silky dress she'd been wearing slipped down her lithe frame. Like innocence embodied she peered at me and slowly stepped out of a black cotton G-string. She looked feather light and graceful. I hardly gave myself time to enjoy the view,, breathing in her scent gently I hoisted her around my waist and with anything, but patience drove into her gripping her soft ass cheeks for leverage.

I'm sure someone in the house heard the first shriek. It was too late to quiet her by the time I forced her against the wall and covered her mouth. But then I released her.

Whatever, let them hear. Everyone in this house was fucking anything that moved. And bringing new things to screw and drink from everyday.

She breathed through her nose, her hands fisted in my hair, her nails biting into my skin. I held her tight against the wall, and pounded myself into her at a brutal pace, the way I've been wanting to for months.

It was a quick, rough, hungry fuck, the only way I did it nowadays.

"Camden," she groaned, her nails digging into my back, "It's been so long."

"Yeah," I smiled against her neck, my hips speeding up.

"It's harder than I remember."

I confessed as I sank into her, "Better too."

She moaned in approval, her grip on my back, my hair, her legs wrapped around me, all surrendered, weak, and willing.

She kissed my lips forcefully as her hands roamed over my body, finally gripping my ass and pulling me deeper inside her. I could feel her stiffen, her nails dig into my skin, her moans more desperate, more needy. Suddenly we were both cumming, a mutual, intense, yearning orgasm.

I was breathing heavily as the waves of pleasure crashed over me, more powerful than I can remember. My heart was pounding, my head spinning. My whole body began to shake and I forced myself to relax my grip on her.

I felt her legs loosen, her arms drop, her body slump against the wall.

"Wow," she breathed, her voice shaking.

I chuckled. "Yeah." I pulled out of her, helping her stand up right, my eyes traveled down her body, to her bare legs, the small pools of shower water on the bathroom floor, to her burnished hair and flushed skin, to her bare chest heaving, a speck of blood on her neck.

"Are you alright?" I asked, rubbing her back.

She shivered, still dazed, and pulled her dress back up over her body, covering herself. "Yeah. I'm fine. But we should probably..."

I furrowed my brow as I picked up her dress, helping her pull the thin material back on. "Yeah. I'll meet you downstairs later."

She nodded as I helped zip up her dress. "But I was wondering, did you maybe want to visit the beach with me later. There are fishing poles in the shed, we could reel 'em in."

I smirked, "You fish?"

"I have."

I squeezed her chin and gave her a soft kiss on the lips. "Maybe we'll see."

Later I took the stairs to the first floor, making my way down the hall to the open kitchen. I paused at the bare marble island.

My eyes settle on A.J checking the pulse of the last blood bank, the man with the crown of fake roses, tattooed around his arm. He was slumped on the sofa in shorts and a shirt, an old C.D player in his lap.

"He must have gotten an infection" A. J said "He was a tough son of a bitch. But if we're gonna keep domesticated donors this way we'd better collect a nice cache of medicine and health kits. " A.J laughed. "He's gone now."

I tried to force myself out of the daze, out of the trance and find some thread of humanity left in my body, but as my jaw creaked open, all that came out of me was, "We'll have to get more."

From behind the sofa, A.J peered at me. "Isn't Payton out?" His eyes slid down my shirtless form, "With Grayson, right? Does that ever bother you?"

I rolled my eyes. "I'll go out later, and see what I can do." Was that me who just planned to go out and hunt humans? Did I say that?

I open the fridge. inside was ten jars of blood and a severed finger. For a split-second normalcy returned and I felt a gag coming on, but it was flushed away with thoughts of the blood sliding down my throat. I grabbed a jar, unscrewed the lid and drank heartily.

"Hey, help me get rid of him would you?" A.J said.

I faltered. I'd touched a human corpse, more times than I'd have liked to admit. But who was the man with the rose crown, what had he been doing here, who loved him? Did I kill him directly or through my intoxicated inaction?

Was that his sweet honey-thick blood I'd just drank?

Taking a deep breath, I joined A.J., trying to suppress my revulsion. The weight of the body was surprising. The cold, lifeless touch sent shivering memories coursing through me.

As we maneuvered the man's body through the beach house, the glass sliding door, and into the backyard, I couldn't help but wonder about the secrets he might be carrying with him to his grave. The night air was cool, and the rhythmic sound of the waves crashing on the shore seemed oddly comforting. It was surreal, hauling a lifeless form towards the sea.

As we rolled him out to the water's edge, I couldn't shake the sense that I was part of something much larger and darker than I had ever imagined. A.J. and I fell into a silence, both lost in thought, watching the body gently slide into the water. It was an eerie moment, the final act of a macabre play that neither of us had chosen to star in. At Least I hadn't

I couldn't help but break the stillness, speaking just above a whisper. "A.J, who do you think this guy was? Why do you think he was here?" I asked, my curiosity gnawing at me, trying to penetrate our darkness with some semblance of importance. The senseless cruelty permeating my life had begun to weigh.

A.J. turned to me, his face etched with a mix of sadness and resignation. "I don't know, wh--. Well, sometimes we're just better off not asking too many questions," he replied, his voice strained. "Maybe if we question ourselves too much, we'll cease to exist eventually—go extinct you know? And besides who cares who he was, who the hell cares who we are in this shit?"

His breath eased out on a blunt exhale. The end of the discussion for us both.

As I turned my gaze about the expanse of the shore, my eyes widened in disbelief.

The moonlight revealed a horrific sight. Over a hundred bodies, similar to the one we had just disposed of, were floating in the ocean, drifting among the waves, illuminated by the silvery glow of the sun.

As I gazed out at the waters, a thought came through with stunning clarity. What the fuck are you doing here?

***

In the middle of the night, a piercing scream shattered my slumber. Heart pounding, I stumbled out of bed, disoriented. My mind raced back to a haunting memory I had tried to bury: Markeya, dying in the McDaniel's living room, her pale blue pajamas stark against the crimson stain of her blood.

My breaths came in ragged gasps as I shot toward the door, scanning the gloomy space around me, I followed the sound. The hallway stretched. I raced down it, and hasten down the carpeted stairs. Light met me as I fell out into the open living area of the house.

My agitated state played tricks on my mind, and I saw Markeya's face on Heather, vulnerable and helpless. In the chaos of the moment, the room's shadows danced, and flickered.

"Keya," I whispered. My trembling hands reached out to pull Payton away, but a strange force held me back. The world spun around me, and I sank under a voracious need to protect Markeya, to save her from a fate I had already been unable to prevent. I reeled back against the wall that pardoned off the kitchen, the living room was in disarray. Shards of the coffee table lay in three big pieces on the floor. But what happened to the chandelier, I thought crazily, as Payton's fang sank into Heather. The McDaniel's had had a chandelier in their destroyed foyer by which the devastation of my life had been revealed to me.

If only she had drank. If only I had made her drink.

If I could've changed her mind.

Her mind was made up.

You don't get to decide what's right for me.

My skin set aflame, reality crashed back in a torrent of raw agony. Markeya was dead, gone. And this was not her I saw but Heather screaming on the living room floor.

Heather's contorted smooth features, wailing in pleading piercing cries. Heather's small hand reached out desperately for me.

Payton gripped Heather's hair and wrenched her head back. Blood poured like a river down Heather's soft creamy throat, soaking the front of her University of Florida sweatshirt until all I could see of the Gator mascot was his grinning snout. Payton's jaw worked on Heather's throat, but her deep green eyes peered fiercely at me shining with blame and wicked madness.

I lept, tearing Payton away from Heather, dragging her back by her throat. She let out a strangle raged-filled howl. Her fangs bared and dripping, and her strength surprising

Heather's protesting cries reached a keen, excruciating pitch.

I grappled Payton for a good minute, pinning her to the living room floor. She reached around me, sharp nails like claws for Heather, killer intent boosted her efforts. Heather crawled back scream-crying. The sound of it, all of it cored through my body until I thought I would blow apart like a powder keg. I twisted the predator in my grasp like a pretzel, until finally I had her facing away from me and pinned her under the arms in a bear hug.

The sun was beginning to rise, casting its first rays of light across the horizon. I held Payton firmly, fury burning in my eyes.

"Payton," I snarled, "For fucks sake what are you doing?

"I'll end it between the two of you," she cried. "If you don't swear right now that you'll never touch her again, I'll kill her."

"Leave Heather alone, Payton. You want to hurt someone, you want to blame somebody? Blame me."

This was my fault. I didn't belong here, didn't account for my presence in this world. Where I thought I had been wallpaper, a symbiotic parasite on the Earth, the truth was I'd been the hurricane force winds tearing it apart. I saw it all around me.

The detriment all around us. The wound on Heather's neck. The floating bodies in the sea. The destroyed living room and then Grayson and A.J pouring out of the downstairs rooms at the spectacle.

Payton turned her head slightly to reach my gaze. "Do you love her?" Fear crept into her expression anticipating my answer. The first light of dawn touched her skin, and she winced, the sunlight scorching her profile.

Under the unforgiving rays, the world around us seemed to lose its luster. Though I had spent months living out the very essence of all human nightmares, I found the truth of my nature amplified by the harsh reality of daybreak.

I'm a vampire, I thought. Finally, the truth came home, and I shuddered under the weight of neck-breaking grief. The aroma of Heather's fear, the sight of her desperate struggles, the touch of her chilled skin beneath my grip, and the metallic taste of regret all swirled in a cacophony of sensations. You'll feel more than you'd ever felt had you been human.

"I'm leaving." I said.

Payton's fear-stricken eyes pleaded with me, and she dared to utter those three words that had become meaningless in the face of our thirst. "I love you," she breathed.

I looked at her but didn't see her. The memories of my lost friends, their laughter, and the love we once shared, mingled with the specter of Markeya, who had graced my life with her vibrant presence, only to be cruelly snatched away.

I remembered the love I had felt for my parents, and then their bitter betrayal which had drawn me into this nightmarish world. Love had become a double-edged sword, inflicting pain as sharply as it delivered pleasure. The more I felt, the more it hurt, and I had learned that the cost of love was simply too high.

My response was not one of warmth but of bitter mockery. "Sure, you do." I scoffed, my heart heavy with regret and anguish. I pushed a lock of her dark hair from her forehead. "We are not capable of love, Payton, only destruction. We're the destroyers of everything that was good about this planet. The only thing we love is blood."

Payton's expression shifted from fear to a resigned sorrow. She recognized the futility of clinging to any semblance of our twisted relationship. When I released her, she retreated. Pushing herself back against the overturned couch. "Fine, go."

I stood under scrutiny of four pairs of eyes.

"The only monster here is you." Payton spat.

The humanity I had clung to had become a fading memory, a casualty of the irresistible allure of human blood. I knew with harrowing clarity that no space to care for anyone, not even myself, remained in my heart.

And with that I slowly turned to stone.

***

The day I returned, I learned Giovanna possessed, quite literally, a certain power to read minds. At least mine.

When I finally made it home, my parents' lavish estate seemed like a mirage on a faraway horizon. I prepared myself to be reprimanded for my escape, but instead, I was met with visitors—men with fangs in military fatigues. A strange emblem glared red and white on their lapels, not the American flag, or any national flag I'd ever seen.

I could tell just from the obvious rapport between the men and my parents that they had worked under or with my dad, but recently or perhaps simultaneously worked for the Kine. The four of them, mom, dad, and the officers waited in the lush sitting area as I entered the front door. All smiles turned my way, just as deceivingly nonconfrontational as those at an intervention.

My father welcomed me into the house and introduced me first to Sergeant Graves, a bald, black man posed stiffly upright on mom's lounge. He stood up and confidently shook my hand.

I'd taken pains to desensitize myself to all emotion for months and in seconds, the stare Graves gave me sent it all spinning back. A shiver raced down my spine. I looked away from him quickly.

"And Sergeant Turner," Sergio went on.

Two sergeants on a home visit? I nearly scoffed at the incredulousness. There must have been a highly specialized assignment for Sergio in the works. Sergeant Turner shook my hand as well, then took his seat next to Graves again.

The men smiled at me and seemed to inspect my stature like horse breeders. My feet were bare, and my hair had grown long. But not long enough to hide a garish undercut in the back, the type that spoiled Hollywood actors designed with spikes and monograms. I was shirtless, clad in stolen designer jeans and a blazer.

"He was just... out there all on his own this whole time?" Turner asked my father.

"What the fuck are you talking about," I interrupted purposely vicious.

Sergio looked mortified but hid it pretty well with clenched teeth.

Giovanna coughed loudly, a glass of white wine in her hand. "Camden. These nice, respected gentlemen visited a few months ago. Around the time you disappeared? --- seeking to recruit you. You weren't here---," she tapered off. I figured she hadn't explained to dad how she did nothing at all to prevent my departure. Besides, what could she have done?

"But as you can see, he is alive." Sergio said. "Which is testament to his constitution in itself. He ran headlong into the hornet's nest, should've come back a few limbs less." I didn't know why but I swore he was bragging about my surviving the escape for a particular reason. "Not a mark on him, isn't that something?"

"Marine Corps?" Turner nodded proudly.

I looked at him curiously. What did these assholes want?

Graves nodded too but then whispered in the ear of Turner.

"You know whispering doesn't work anymore." I called boldly. "I heard you. And yes, I did just end a month-long bender."

Sergio laughed nervously. It became apparent that they were here to draft me into the war against humans; a war that I did not understand but could not escape from either. And it was even more clear that my parents wanted these two men to think I was a good candidate. A loyal supporter of... I didn't know what. And I didn't know why.

"The first few days of thirst," Graves said carefully, "Are hard for everyone, son, it's fine whatever you've done to get by. We're not here to judge."

"That's right," Sergio said, clapping my shoulder. "But we do have to get you back on track. What we want is your stability again, the Kine's army will do that. The Kine will take care of you."

"I don't need to be taken care of, thanks."

"No, you need blood." Graves said, stopping everything inside me. "We can help with that, a steady and safe supply of the cleanest, fullest human blood the world has to offer and all you have to do is stay loyal to your kind."

Whatever the hell that meant, it mattered almost not at all to me. Part of me wanted to cry tears of joy, part of me wanted to leave again. But what would become of me if I left now? Back out there in the thick of it. I needed the blood and the justification they offered.

***

"Don't you want to be a soldier again?" my father asked, gripping a rake and sweeping up the charred remains of the animal carcasses some strangers left on our front lawn. I felt like a person filled to the brim with cement as I stared down at what looked like a destroyed stuffed raccoon.

"I am a soldier." I answered.

"But how would you like to serve again?"

I shook my head and held out the leaf bag. "Serve what?" I said, there's no Earth left, no people left to protect. My fury burned inside. Markeya's face flashed across my mental screen, and I had to use all the strength I could muster to stay upright. Giovanna would only allow me a pint of blood per week and that wasn't enough to blunt the images. All the pain was trickling back in like venom.

"Us, your kind," Sergio answered, "The Kine's purpose is to establish a safer, more harmonious society as quickly as possible. And of course, there are some obstacles to that. In this case the obstacles are enormous. We'll need all the help we can----."

"Fuck no." I grumbled and felt anger like boiling water in my throat.

Sergio paused, smiled.

The look of his fangs behind his lips mixed with the hot greasy smell of the animal carcass on the rake. It made me want to vomit. The sickness of these creatures,

Burning animals on the lawns of the neighborhood, filling the oceans and the streets with the dead. Feigns have taken over the world.

Sergio dumped the pile into the lawn bag for disposal. I double knotted it.

"You're still mad about your friends huh?" he said, as if asking about my intended major in college, or what new movie was playing in theaters.

"Mad?" I stood up straight, furious. I planted my gaze on him. "Did you ask if I was mad?" My best friend and the love of my life were murdered and he thought I was mad. "Markeya, might have been pregnant." I said swallowing.

Though his body seemed to go rigid, I knew even then he would not acknowledge the information. No matter how devastating, how destructive and tragic the effects, remaining emotionally unaware was the only way to get what he wanted from me.

"They aren't coming back, Camden, and now you have a decision to make. You can either accept and anticipate an immortal under the Kine. Or." My father pulled a chrome handgun from his waistband and held it out for me. "You can get it over with now."

I thought about it. I thought long and I thought hard. Though my grabbing the gun and firing at him hadn't been his intention, I saw it happen with a painful, nearly irresistible realism. But I couldn't, not yet. "Maybe later." I told him and mys

Get bonus content, freebie giveaways and exclusive details on upcoming books in The Dark Reunion Series.

Check it out now at: authortishthomas.com

- Follow me on Instagram:

https://www.instagram/Tish.writes.vampires

- Follow me on Twitter:

@Tishparanormal

- Check out my Facebook page:

https://www.Facebook.com/TishWritesFiction

Thank you for reading The Dark Reunion Series by Tish Thomas